BILLIONAIRE'S CLUB

BILLIONAIRE'S CLUB CAST OF CHARACTERS

HEROES AND HEROINES:

Abigail Roberts (Bad Night Stand) — founding member of the Sextant, hates wine, loves crocheting

Jordan O'Keith (Bad Night Stand) — Heather's brother, former owner of RoboTech

Cecilia (CeCe) Thiele (Bad Breakup) — former nanny to Hunter, talented artist

Colin McGregor (Bad Breakup) — Scottish duke, owner of McGregor Enterprises

Heather O'Keith (Bad Husband) — CEO of RoboTech, Jordan's sister

Clay Steele (Bad Husband) — Heather's business rival, CEO of Steele Technologies

Kay (Bad Date) — romance writer, hates to be stood up

Garret Williams (Bad Date) — former rugby player

Rachel Morris (Bad Hookup) — Heather's assistant, superpowers include being ultra-organized

Sebastian (Bas) Scott (Bad Hookup) — Devon Scott's brother, Clay's assistant

Rebecca (Bec) Darden (Bad Divorce) — kickass lawyer, New York roots

Luke Pearson (Bad Divorce) — Southern gentleman, CEO Pearson Energies

Seraphina Delgado (Bad Fiancé) — romantic to the core, looks like a bombshell, but even prettier on the inside

Tate Connor (Bad Fiancé) — tech genius, scared to be burned by love

Lorelai (Bad Text) — drunk texts don't make her happy

Logan Smith (Bad Text) — former military, sometimes drunk texts are for the best

Kelsey Scott (Bad Boyfriend) — Bas and Devon's sister, engineer at RoboTech, brilliant

Tanner Pearson (Bad Boyfriend) — Bas and Devon's childhood friend, photographer

Trix Donovan (Bad Blind Date) — Heather's sister, Jordan's half-sister, nurse who worked in war zones, poverty-stricken areas, and abroad for almost a decade

Jet Hansen (Bad Blind Date) — a doctor Trix worked with

Molly Miller (Bad Wedding) — owner of Molly's, a kickass bakery in San Francisco

Jackson Davis (Bad Wedding) — Molly's ex-fiancé

Kate McLeod (Bad Engagement) — Kelsey's college friend, advertiser extraordinaire, loves purple and Hermione Granger

Jaime Huntingon (Bad Engagement) — vet, does excellent man-bun

Heidi Greene (Bad Bridesmaid) — science, organization, and *Twilight* nerd

Brad Huntington (Bad Bridesmaid) — travel junkie, dreamy hazel eyes, hidden sweet side

Ben Bradford (Bad Swipe) — quiet, brooding, had a thing for golden retrievers

Stef McKay (*Bad Swipe*) — lab assistant, dog lover, klutzy to the extreme
Tammy Huntington (*Bad Girlfriend*) — allergic to relationships
Fletcher King (*Bad Girlfriend*) — has a thing for smart, sassy women

Additional Characters:

George O'Keith — Jordan's dad
Hunter O'Keith — Jordan's nephew
Bridget McGregor — Colin's mom
Lena McGregor — Colin's sister
Bobby Donovan — Heather's half and Trix's full brother
Frances and Sugar Delgado — Sera's parents
Devon Scott — Kels and Bas's brother
Becca Scott — Kels and Bas's sister in law
Heidi Greene — Kels' friend since college
Cora Hutchins — Kels' friend since childhood
Fred — the bestest golden retriever in the world*Sir Fuzzy McFeatherston aka The Fuzz* — Jaime and Kate's pet rooster

To those of us who wear armor and lock our hearts up in steel chests.
Don't be afraid to relinquish the key.

ONE

Bec

BEC CLOSED the file she'd been working on and stretched her arms above her head. Her shoulders ached, her eyes burned—she'd gone way over the thirty minutes of continuous computer screen time her optometrist recommended—and she was the absolute last person left in the building.

Seriously.

Security had come by her office an hour earlier, telling her they'd locked up and the high-rise was empty.

Except for her.

She probably should have been lonely, being the singular human presence around, but Bec loved this time of night. It was after one, and she'd been in the office since six the previous morning working on a case she was preparing for trial.

But fuck, did she love finding a legal loophole in a contract and being the one to decisively close it.

Nothing was better than that.

Not being made partner several months before. Not the money or the power. Not having a slew of paralegals whose job it was to go line by line through all the paperwork pertaining to her cases and find loopholes like the one she'd just spent hours scouring for.

Those were all intoxicating in many ways.

But still, nothing topped the law itself.

The different interpretations, the way it morphed based on a court's or judge's decision, how it changed from year to year. Even finding this particular loophole after all the others before her had failed sent her pulse thundering.

One lawyer to rule them all.

Snorting at her inner SciFi nerd—not that she'd had much spare time to indulge in any form of hobby as of late . . . okay, as of the last ten years, if she were being honest—Bec knew it was all worth it. Law was her first love, and it was a constantly shifting spider's web, a fragile and intricate and complex lover.

But it also made sense to her when so many other things in her world did not.

"And now I've killed my own buzz," she muttered before logging off her computer, grabbing a stack of files from her desk, shoving them into her briefcase, and then slipping on her suit jacket and black pumps.

Down the elevator, through the locked door to the garage, and into her car.

Quiet.

So quiet.

She'd grown up in New York—or at least spent enough of her formative years in the Big Apple for her accent to reflect her time there—and felt more comfortable in big cities. San Francisco was a nice metropolis, but it had a definite sleepy time . . . or at least the district where her office was located did.

Normally, she liked that, preferred it over the way New York had always buzzed with activity.

But Bec had been . . . feeling weird as of late.

She was used to city life—the expensive rents, the exhaust fumes that hung in the air at all hours of the day, the horns and sirens and screeching brakes.

But this quiet? Fuck, did it hit her straight in the gut.

Or maybe it wasn't the quiet so much as *disquiet?*

Bec was a simple woman. She didn't censor herself, didn't trouble over hurt feelings or someone's toes being stepped on. She took care of business in the quickest, most efficient way possible.

That was Rebecca Darden. What she was famous for—at least in the legal world.

No prisoners. Decisive. Smart as hell and not a fucking pushover.

She'd spent a lifetime studying and working and losing sleep and clawing and fighting and struggling against the pressures of being in a male-dominated field to become that woman.

And yet . . .

"Fuck," she said and turned on her car, making her way through the quiet city to her apartment. "I'm losing it."

Because she couldn't help but feel that even though she'd finally met her goal of being partner, of being revered and feared and even sometimes reviled—all fine qualities in her opinion— that she was missing out on something.

There.

She'd said it.

Rebecca *Fucking* Darden felt that somehow along the way to all her success she'd missed out on *something.*

Unfortunately, she couldn't figure out what the fuck that *something* was.

A bigger challenge?

Nope. A month before, she'd taken on a case with impossible odds and had just that evening figured out how to win it.

Longer hours?

Hell no. At this point, she was paying for an apartment she was hardly ever in.

More money? No. She already had an obscene amount.

Better relationship with her father? Nope. Things were . . . well, at this point, she'd pretty much given up hope for a happy ending in that sector.

Different friends?

No fucking way. Her group of women—and now a few men —were the shit. They kept her sane and laughed at her jokes and were really incredible people.

She loved them, and *that* was saying something, especially coming from her and her limited tolerance of bullshit. She didn't like easy, let alone *love* easily.

And she loved every one of them.

So . . . *what?*

That was the fucking problem. She *didn't* know. Normally, she'd just turn a particular puzzle over in her mind until she figured it out, as she'd done with the contract that evening.

But she'd been turning this freaking enigma over in her mind for months, and Bec was no closer to discovering the exact source of her unease.

"Boo fucking hoo," she murmured, pulling into her parking spot and making it up to her floor via her private elevator. The lift went directly to her penthouse—yes, the apartment she hardly spent any time in was a ridiculously expensive penthouse that required a series of codes to access it.

Because of that private elevator, Bec didn't expect to see another person waiting for her when the doors opened with a soft *ding* and she stepped off.

But there *was* another person waiting just outside her front door.

A person she never expected to see again.

Luke Pearson.

Her ex-husband.

It was one-fucking-thirty in the morning, and her ex-husband was sitting on the floor outside her apartment.

Asleep.

Fuming, she marched over to him and kicked his shoe. Hard.

"Luke," she snapped. "Why in the ever-loving fuck are you here?"

His lids peeled back, sleepy green eyes met hers. "Becky," he murmured. "You're gorgeous as always." The drowsiness began to fade from his expression. "Did you just come from work?" He glanced down at his phone. "Do you know what time it is?"

"Of course I know what time it is—" Bec bit back the rest of her words. Fuck, but wasn't this conversation an exact replica of the broken record they'd played *way* too many times over the course of their relationship?

She crossed her arms. "Never mind that." She shot him a glare that had withered balls much bigger than Luke's. "Why did you break into my apartment?"

He stood, towering over her. Once, Bec would have said that his size made her feel petite, feminine, soft, which was atypical for a giant Amazon such as herself. Today, it just pissed her off. She was tall for a woman, almost six feet in heels, and was used to using that fact to her advantage.

No longer hunching her shoulders to appear shorter. Hell, no. She wore heels if she wanted and as high as she wanted—

And she had this man to thank for that fact.

"Stand tall, sugar pie," he used to say.

Yes, Luke had called her—world-famous, tough as shit lawyer—*sugar pie*.

But that had been a long time ago, when she'd been broken and . . .

Her heart, the one she liked to pretend didn't actually exist, pulsed with old hurt.

Because she'd merely been an entertaining side project for him, a broken toy to fix, a puzzle to figure out and one to discard when he couldn't find a satisfactory answer.

Memories.

Aw.

Motherfucking memories.

"First, I didn't break into your apartment. This is the hall. Second," he hurried to add when she opened her mouth to argue semantics, "I didn't break in. You used our anniversary as the code."

Oh, for fuck's sake.

Well, she was changing that tomorrow . . . today . . . fuck, *yesterday*, now that—

"Go away, Luke," she said, pushing past him and unlocking her door while blocking his view of the keypad that was identical to that of the elevator. Her front door's code was *not* the date of her anniversary with her ex.

But Luke probably already knew that, given that he had been sitting on the floor of her hallway rather than on her couch, beer in hand, feet making prints on her glass coffee table.

Men.

Fucking men.

She slammed the door closed behind her and secured the chain lock. The knock approximately one second later did not surprise her. Bec dropped her briefcase to the floor then opened the door just enough to shoot angry eyes at him through the narrow gap the chain allowed.

Serious green eyes fixed onto hers. "We need to talk."

"Luke," she snapped. "I'm exhausted. It's the middle of the

night. I wouldn't have any patience to talk to my best friends right now, let alone my ex-husband."

"Funny story about that," he said, his lips curving. "Turns out that I'm not actually your *ex*-husband."

TWO

Luke

HE YAWNED and rubbed a hand over his mouth, neck aching, head pounding, back stiff as shit.

Man, he was getting old if he was sore just from sleeping.

Except . . . he opened his eyes and finally clued into awareness.

His Becky had always said he was slow.

His lips twitched. Because he'd loved nothing more than when his Becky gave him sass. Luke pulled out his cell from his pocket, checked the time, and grinned as he pushed to his feet outside her apartment. He'd fallen asleep in the hallway, after listening to Becky moving around inside, probably fixing a cup of tea, slipping into a pair of those silky, stupidly expensive pajamas she loved, and finally padding on quiet feet to the door, no doubt to check if he'd gone.

Luke had shifted to the side by then, well out of sight of the peephole, so he'd heard those soft footfalls hesitate by the door before they'd retreated back into what he presumed was her bedroom.

Then his imagination had gone to work, or further R-rated work anyway, picturing Becky sliding between satin sheets, stripping off those silken pajamas, reaching a hand down between her thighs—

Yes, he was a sick bastard.

No, he didn't give a damn.

Regardless, it was early, barely six, and so Luke was in prime position to get a jump on Becky. It had been after two before she'd headed to bed, and even his workaholic of a woman wouldn't already be in the office. Plus, he'd slept here so she *couldn't* avoid him again. He'd get her to talk to him, get her good and mad so she couldn't ignore him.

Because while it might have been a decade since he'd seen his Becky, Luke had never forgotten her.

Never gotten over her.

Never regretted something as much as letting her go.

Yes, they'd been young and stupid and beyond immature at twenty-five. They'd had no business getting married, and he'd had no right to be hurt that the woman he'd loved was a go-getter.

Becky had more drive in one of her pinky fingers than most people had in their entire lives.

That work ethic wasn't common amongst their kind.

Kids with rich parents, who never wanted for anything, who always had the best clothes and cars and toys.

But they'd also been just kids.

Kids who'd wanted nothing more than their parents' attention and kids who'd been shipped off to boarding school. They craved attention and love more than anything, and they hadn't been able to find it at home.

Or maybe that was just Luke.

Except . . . once upon a time it had been Becky, too.

He rubbed a hand over his face and stood, trying to shove

those memories down. He'd been hurt, *so fucking hurt*, Becky had left—even though he'd done his best to push her away—that he'd signed the papers.

Divorce papers.

Super smart.

But that was Luke.

Make him mad enough, and he'd do stupid shit without a second thought.

Or, that was *usually* the case—a lack of second thoughts—but despite his best efforts, Luke *hadn't* forgotten Becky. Not then, not now, not ever. He'd had plenty of regrets. And when he found out the small county courthouse Becky had filed for divorce in had burned down, that their paperwork hadn't ever been fully processed, Luke had hoped.

For the first time in forever, he'd hoped.

His father was dead, his mother was busy traveling the world, and his sister was happily married.

Luke's life consisted of him . . . and the oil company. And while he'd enjoyed the challenge of running the family business, Pearson Energy, had loved spending the five years since his father's passing converting the company's focus from fossil fuels to renewable solar and wind sources, it wasn't enough.

Yes, he'd sound like a fucking pussy admitting this, but he was lonely.

And no woman could compare to Becky.

Not his former fiancée (and the reason he'd discovered he was still married to one Rebecca Darden), not the string of girlfriends and one-night stands from the last ten years.

Becky was it for him, and he'd been a fool to try to pretend otherwise.

Sighing, he reached out a hand to knock on her door. He'd let her escape the previous evening—earlier that morning—

because she'd had dark circles under her eyes and a hint of panic in her expression.

Like one of his horses.

His mouth curved, knowing Becky would definitely hate that comparison, and he shifted, readying himself to knock again.

That was the moment he heard the crinkle.

Luke glanced down and his stomach dropped.

A note.

Another fucking note.

His temper spiked as he bent to pick it up then it flared to molten, furious attention when he unfolded the paper and read the contents.

Go home, Luke. You know we only make each other
miserable.
-Bec
P.S. I changed the code.
P.P.S. Next time you try to hang out and "surprise" me,
consider the fact that there's a camera in this hallway.
P.P.P.S. Route any documentation regarding our former
marriage to my office at McAvoy, Darden, and
Associates.

"Go home," he muttered, knocking once more to no answer, listening for sounds of movement inside before conceding that he'd lost this round. Becky must have slipped past him.

He headed for the elevator, punched the down button.

"Go. Home," he repeated.

He'd done that before.

And it had been the biggest mistake of his life.

Luke might be a lot of things—stubborn, stupid, and worse—

but he didn't repeat his mistakes. He learned from them, and so .
. . no, he wasn't going to leave.

His lips curved into a wicked smile. Besides, in her note,
Becky had all but told him to visit her at work.

Nope. Luke wasn't going anywhere.

THREE

Bec

SHE DRANK GREEDILY from her mug of coffee, wishing her bloodstream could immediately absorb the caffeine.

No sleep made for a grumpy Bec.

Especially when the cause of her lack of sleep was Luke fucking Pearson.

Her ex-husband.

Or not, according to him.

"Bullshit," she muttered, scowling as she strode down the hall and into her office. The few enterprising interns who'd began to mirror her work schedule—in early, leave late—skittered out of her path, eyes going wide, and the non-tired, non-muddled-by-Luke portion of her brain forced herself to suck in a breath and relax the lines.

The Darden glare wasn't needed at six in the morning.

Despite Luke and despite the fact that she'd stayed up all night, watching the camera, waiting for her ex to leave or at least fall asleep so she could run.

She never ran.

Except from Luke.

Sighing, she shut the door behind her then sank down into her desk chair. Her office was plush, a visual representation of the thousands of hours she'd spent clawing her way to partner in one of the top employment law offices in the nation.

She'd focused on employment law because of an unpleasant incident at her first internship.

For lawyers, they'd been really fucking stupid.

The disparity between the hours she'd put in and the opportunities she'd been given versus those of her male coworkers had been so big it was almost hysterical.

Billionaire tech-founder for a father or not, Bec had busted her ass. And ultimately, her father didn't really matter, not when the other interns—all male, as she was the only female— each came from equally powerful families.

Yes, she was privileged to have been given the internship at a prestigious firm in the first place, but that was pretty much where any advantage had ended for her.

She'd spent the better part of three months twiddling her thumbs in her cubicle.

Until she'd watched one too many of her male colleagues be pulled into an important meeting with a higher up or invited out for drinks or given an opportunity to work on an interesting case.

She'd been invited to get coffee.

Seriously.

Top of her class at Harvard Law during her first two years, and she'd been regulated to coffee pickup.

Which would have been fine, she didn't mind paying her dues, and she'd be lying if she said she didn't send interns out for coffee regularly, but she made sure *all* her interns took a turn at the underling stuff and that they *all* got a chance with the big, interesting cases.

But ultimately, her not-so-fun internship had been a good thing. It had shifted her focus from corporate to employment law. She'd graduated number one in her class, and then passed the bar on her first try.

And because she was done with privilege, she'd applied for jobs under her mother's maiden name. No more hanging on Daddy's coattails, no more opportunities because of his connections.

Nope. She'd made her own way.

And Luke had been by her side the whole time. They'd met at boarding school, friends then lovers then, unbeknownst to both of their families, they'd become husband and wife.

He'd moved with her when she'd gotten into Harvard, had gotten accepted into the business school there, readying himself to take over his family's company.

He was driven, sexy, and he got her.

He loved that she was tough, that she didn't take any shit.

Until he hadn't.

Ugh.

"Nice, Bec," she muttered. "Nice little trip down a fucked-up memory lane." She set her coffee down and booted up her computer, shoving all thoughts of Luke deep down, back in the locked box in the depths of her heart, icing it over and throwing some barbed wire on top for good measure.

It was airtight, with more security than Fort Knox, and she knew no feelings would dare escape.

She had work and friends.

You have work. Only work. You don't care about anything else.

The thoughts were in Luke's deep drawl and thoroughly unwelcome. He didn't know her. Not any longer. She worked long hours because she loved it, but she also had a life outside the office.

She was fine.

Hell, she was even a godmother to Abby's baby, Emma.

That was something.

That was something normal, not something a cold, robotic, work-a-holic—

And damn, why, after a full decade, did those words still hurt?

Because they'd been shouted at her by the one man she'd opened her heart to, the one man she'd loved and been vulnerable to, and—

Yeah, *that*.

Sighing, she took another sip of coffee and settled down to work, pushing Luke from her mind, shoving away all thoughts that didn't revolve around their doomed marriage, and focusing on what had become her one true love over the years.

The law.

Bec dove headfirst into the safe puzzle of the law.

THE KNOCK at the door wasn't welcome.

It must still be early if someone was knocking at all, because her secretary knew that a closed door meant no freaking interruptions.

None.

None.

But before Bella was in, sometimes people forgot.

New people.

Annoying people.

"Come in," she growled, when the knock came for a second time, the idiot on the other side not recognizing that a closed door and no answer meant *go the fuck away.* She kept eyes focused on the screen, fingers hovering over the keys, typing paused midsentence as she waited for the intruder to speak.

When they didn't, she finished her sentence, sighed, and glanced up.

Then nearly knocked over her coffee.

Luke was inside her office, leaning against the closed door, paper bag in one hand, tray with two cups in the other.

That wasn't the worst part.

Nope, the really horrible, terrible, *awful* part was the expression on his face. Soft and almost gentle, with the slightest smile on his lips. It called to that part of her locked deep within, despite the ice and barbwire and steel-reinforced rebar. That paired with the curl of brown hair falling across his forehead, his biceps bulging under the sleeves of his black T-shirt, and his jeans . . . well, he'd filled out in the last decade because his thighs . . .

Thick, muscular, and *yum*. Her own thighs reacted to the sight, squeezing together, a hint of dampness in between.

Just from a look.

Fuck.

Her body still remembered his.

And he knew it, based on the way his mouth curved into a sinful—and egotistical—grin.

He was beautiful, and he also knew *that*.

Which, luckily for her, was enough for her to remember the past, to remind her who she was in the present—that she was tough and smart and didn't fall for cocky assholes.

You'd like a little cock—

Enough.

She was Rebecca Darden. She didn't cower or avoid. She faced shit head on, and she was certainly strong enough to face her ex-husband.

"Luke."

His brows rose at the icy tone, but it didn't seem to have any other effect on him. He didn't turn and leave like any other man would have done in his place. Instead, he pushed off the door, rose to his full height—still six-foot-three but no longer the lanky boy from the past—and crossed over to her desk.

After plunking the tray and bag on the wooden surface, he sank into the armchair across from her.

"Becky."

Her temper pulsed. "It's Bec."

He stared at her, raised a brow. "Bec," he repeated, and she tried to ignore the fact that it didn't sound right coming from his lips.

She wasn't his Becky anymore.

She waited for him to say anything else, perhaps to explain why he'd intruded on her at work, barreling through her office defenses, interrupting her morning.

But instead, he just sat silently in that chair.

Stifling a sigh, Bec turned her attention back to the brief on her screen, going back a few sentences, trying to remember her place so she could find her flow again. Luke was perhaps as stubborn as she was and, her lawyer skills aside, she'd never been able to pry information out of him.

Wait and see.

That was the only tactic that worked with him.

Wait and see if his disappointment grew.

Wait and see his back when he'd reached his limit and walked away.

She got it. She was a hard sell for most guys, difficult and not a woman to cut anyone any slack, but Luke was supposed to have been different.

She had been different with him.

And it hadn't mattered.

Enough.

Bec reread the sentences again, found the place she'd left off, and with another stifled sigh, she pushed on with her work. It was challenging at first, but after a few tooth-pulling sentences, she managed to find her focus, and pretty soon she was absorbed in the case again, fingers pounding across the keyboard, words filling up the screen, and . . . then she was done.

Stretching her neck from side to side, she saved the document then leaned back in her chair.

Her breath caught in her throat.

Because Luke was watching her.

Part of her brain had known he hadn't left, but that had been a distant part, and she certainly hadn't expected him to be *staring* at her while she'd worked. She could have imagined him waiting her out while scrolling through his cell phone, but studying her as though she were the most intricate, fascinating snarl of law language he'd ever encountered?

No.

Not that. *Never* that.

"Why are you here, Luke?"

"I've missed you."

Crack went the ice around her heart.

FOUR

Luke

HE'D SPENT close to an hour watching Becky work, memorizing the little frown between her eyebrows, fingers itching to smooth back the lock of her hair that had slipped free of her ponytail.

Luke used to tuck those strands behind her ear, used to trail his hand along her neck, loving the way she'd shivered at the touch.

Eventually, she glanced up at him, eyes going a little wide, lush lips parting.

"Why are you here, Luke?"

He told her the truth. "I've missed you."

For a second, he thought she might tell him that she missed him, too, that the decade apart wasn't actually a huge barrier between them being together in the here and now.

Then her face locked down. "No."

"No?" He raised a brow.

"No." Becky popped to her feet, started pacing. "No, you don't miss me. You *can't* miss me. It's been ten years without a word, Luke." She stopped at the window, facing away from him, hands on her hips. "What?" she asked, whipping around to face him. "You saw the article in the *New York Times* about my work and decided to fuck with me? Or maybe the Pearson family business needs an influx of cash? Have you managed to run it into the ground in just five years?"

God, this woman could take him from zero to livid in under one second.

A heartbeat before, he'd been admiring her beauty, the soft lines of her lips and jaw, and now he . . . well, he was still admiring her lines, except he wanted to bend her over her desk and admire the curved lines of her ass or kneel between her thighs and admire the *lines* of her pussy with his tongue.

Except, then he processed her words. *Five years*.

His temper eased.

His mouth curved. "How'd you know I've been running Pearson Energy for five years?"

Becky's shoulders went stiff. "What?"

Luke stood, walked over to her. "You've been keeping tabs on me."

"Fuck no," she snapped, crossing her arms. "I've been busy living my own life, not pining after you." But her eyes didn't meet his. Instead, they slid to the side, focusing on some point over his left shoulder.

Gotcha.

One step closer. Near enough to smell the familiar scent of her. Peaches and bourbon. The south in one inhalation, even though she was a Yankee.

"You're even more beautiful than I remembered."

Her breath caught.

He pressed his advantage. "I should have never let you go."

Lips parted, eyes went soft.

He brushed the backs of his knuckles across her cheek. "I was an ass."

Truth, but also the wrong thing to say, because the moment his words processed, Becky's face went hard and she started to turn away.

Luke caught her arm. "We were good together, sweetheart."

A scoff. "Like oil and water."

"No, like *forever*." He shook his head. "If I hadn't been such an idiot, we would still be together. We were forever, sugar pie."

Becky yanked her arm free, marched over to her desk. She scooped up one of the coffees, brought it her lips, and guzzled the now-cooled drink. Then she peered into the paper bag and froze.

He crossed back over to her, leaned a hip next to her on the desk. "I remembered."

Her sweet tooth. That she'd rather have chocolate for breakfast because it contained the same number of calories as a coffee cake or bagel with shmear or—

She rolled down the top of the bag and shoved it away. "You need to leave. I looked at my records last night. Everything was signed and filed correctly."

"Of course, it was," he told her. "That was never even a question." She was an excellent lawyer and there was never any doubt she'd crossed her T's and dotted her I's. "The issue wasn't with your paperwork, but rather that the county courthouse burned down."

Finally, her gaze rose to meet his.

"Because of the fire, the paperwork was never processed. And according to Carey County Texas"—where Pearson Energy was headquartered, where they'd gone down to his local church and had a secret wedding—"we're still married."

Those pretty gray eyes widened. "How would you even find that out?"

And now it was Luke's turn to not look at her. His eyes skittered away, one hand came up to rub the back of his neck. "I was engaged," he admitted, daring to glance back at her.

Dimmed.

Any lightness in her expression disappeared, just flicked away as effortlessly as though someone had flipped a switch.

"Ah. And so I'm in the way of your latest conquest," she said, coolly. "What is she? Porn star? B-list movie actress? No, it had to be a supermodel."

Considering Luke *had* dated all of those over the last decade, he couldn't exactly fault her logic. There was also the fact that Tiffani—yes, Tiffani with an *I*—*had* been a model. She was also a jewelry designer and an entrepreneur, and successful in her own right.

She just wasn't Becky.

And luckily, he'd discovered that *before* the actual wedding.

Becky read the truth on his face.

"Ah," she said, a smirk curving her mouth. "I'm right. A model."

"Tiffani is very talented," he said, feeling obliged to stick up for his former fiancée. She was a beautiful woman, both on the inside and out, and incredibly sweet.

They'd gone down to pull their marriage license from the courthouse a week before their wedding, only to be informed that he was still married.

Shock. Embarrassment. Then . . . relief.

That he didn't have to marry Tiffani.

Yes, he was a fucking asshole to have felt that way, but it had also lined the pieces up in his mind, fitted them together in perfect symmetry for the first time in an eternity.

"Tiffani," Becky muttered and rounded her desk, putting the block of wood between them. "I'll put something together, make sure it indemnifies us both monetarily for the last decade."

Her gaze met his. "No spousal support, no properties to separate. It'll be quick and painless and get you back to your *Tiffani*."

"No."

One brow rose. "*No?*"

Luke strode around the desk, getting very close to her,
loving that her lips parted slightly when he was near. It gave
him hope that somewhere deep inside her, she might still feel
something for him, that she wasn't as cool and detached as she
was pretending to be.

Of course, it also made him want to kiss her.

"No," he said again. "Pushing you away was the biggest
mistake of my life. Now that I have you again, I'm not letting
you go."

Her hands plunked onto her hips. "But here's the thing,
Pearson, you *don't* have me."

"Maybe not." He held her gaze, saw the flicker in those gray
depths.

"So, I'll take care of the filing, and—"

"*No.*"

The tops of her cheekbones went bright red; fury flickered
across her eyes.

"I don't want a divorce, sugar pie," he said. "I want to give us
another try."

Becky exploded into motion, shoving him back, moving past
him . . . or trying to anyway. He snagged her wrist.
"Sweetheart—"

"No," she snapped this time. "*No.* You don't get to throw me
away like trash and then just waltz back into my life. You don't
get to decide that because all your other options didn't work out,
you'll return for your leftovers." She jerked her wrist out of his
grip. "I'm worth more. I *deserve* more. I don't need you in my
life, Luke. I really fucking don't."

"I know."

That froze her in place.

"*I* need you."

Her jaw dropped open as he closed the distance between them. "But if you can convince me that you really don't feel anything for me, that your life is perfectly fulfilled without me, then I'll go." He ignored the fire in her gaze and gently touched her cheek. "I'll let that door hit me on the ass and sign whatever pieces of paper you send my way."

She lifted her chin, opened her mouth—

"*If* you can convince me that you feel nothing."

She stiffened and jerked away. "Of all the disgusting, egotistical, asinine things I've ever heard. *I* have to convince *you*? I don't *have* to do a damn thing, Pearson."

Fuck, but he loved when she called him by his last name.

But he couldn't let that distract him. Not when he had Becky where he wanted her, not when she would sense such a vulnerability and take ruthless advantage.

Luke crossed his arms. "Then, I stay."

"*Ugh!*" She threw her hands up. "What then, Luke? What do you want from me?"

"A kiss."

Becky stilled. "What?"

"One kiss. You don't feel anything, and I'll leave," he said. "But if you *do* feel something, I get to stay for a while."

Gray eyes narrowed. "How long's a *while*?"

"Ten dates. One to make up for every year I fucked up. I get to choose the days, times, and locations. I'll work around your schedule," he added when she started to protest. "But you'll have to promise to not purposely block or avoid me. At the end of it, if you decide that you've had enough of me, I'll leave. No negotiations, no fight."

Her brows pulled together for a moment before relaxing. "Fine. Not that the terms matter, since your little experiment won't prove anything. One kiss, which will be nothing, and you'll leave, sign whatever I send to you."

"One kiss," he agreed, "and I'll sign. But *I* get to kiss *you*. No cheater smack of your lips against my cheek, like you'd kiss a child."

Her face fell before she could hide it, and Luke was glad he'd thought of and closed that particular loophole.

Silence then a heavy sigh. "Fine. But when I don't feel anything, you'll go."

"Deal." He extended his hand.

She placed her palm in his. "De—"

He tugged, knowing he had to act before she had time to erect all her defenses against him. The movement brought her close, her front pressed tightly to his, her mouth mere centimeters from his. Gray eyes darkened, lips flushed pink. Wisps of her blonde hair escaped her ponytail and curled around her face. Luke watched her blink, knew he couldn't let her regain herself, couldn't let that control reappear.

Sex had never been their issue. Their chemistry was off the charts, and he was affected by their proximity himself, considering he was rocking a boner like a sixteen-year-old.

But Becky was smart and strong and stubborn as fuck. To win this battle, she'd suppress even the most overwhelming need.

In this one moment, Luke needed to be smarter, stronger, *more* stubborn.

Because this was his shot.

And he wouldn't get another chance.

He bent, flicked his tongue against her lower lip. Becky jerked, lips parting, and Luke took his chance. He pressed his mouth to hers.

Heat.

Sparks.

Right.

He angled her jaw, lining up their lips, slipping his tongue inside to tangle with hers. She stiffened, staying lax, and his gut clenched. It was a Hail Mary, pure panic on his part to snap her out of herself that prompted him to nip her bottom lip. She jumped, stiff for one long heartbeat before she melted against him, breasts flush against his chest, soft curves he was desperate to caress.

But he'd promised one kiss.

And nowadays, he kept his promises.

He slipped his tongue back between her lips, finally coaxing hers to dance intimately with his. Her hands came up, wrapping around his neck and finally, *finally* she let herself be taken over by the kiss.

Victory and relief flooded through him in equal waves.

But he knew he couldn't let himself completely lose his mind. He needed to stay sharp with his Becky or he'd lose the biggest gamble of his life.

So he pulled back way before he wanted to, loving that her eyes had slid closed, that her body listed toward his. Luke cupped her cheek and pressed one more kiss to her forehead before stepping away.

"Not unaffected," he said softly. "I win."

Lids flashed open, reddened lips parted to speak—

"I'll call you," he said and high-tailed it out of Becky's office, closing the door behind him.

This thing with Becky wasn't one battle.

It was a war. And in war, a man had to know when to make a strategic retreat.

He had ten dates to plan.

FIVE

Bec

SHE STARED, stunned and beyond turned on, at the closed door to her office.

What in the fuck had just happened?

Bec sighed, returned to her chair on shaky legs—not that she would ever admit such a thing to *anyone*—and sank down into the plush leather.

"Luke Pearson happened," she muttered. "The low-down, sneaky bastard."

Except . . . he hadn't kissed like a bastard.

"Ugh." She pounded a few keys on her computer, opening her email and weeding through her inbox while stewing on the problem that was her ex. She cleared everything important before pulling up a browser and searching for the number for the Carey County clerk.

One glance at her clock showed her that with the two-hour time change, they should be open, and so she dialed the number.

Two rings, one ten-minute conversation with a very friendly employee—way more friendly than her local California office—

and Luke's story had been confirmed. The courthouse had burned down, all in-house records were lost, and because they hadn't yet switched to having files backed up electronically, anything that was in the middle of being processed there had been lost.

Everything that had been stored off-site was fine and *those* documents were now in the electronic system.

Which meant that according to Carey County, they were still married.

Even though she had paperwork that said she'd filed for divorce ten years before.

Sigh.

It would really be a simple fix to push through a divorce now. No judge would deny them, not with the papers signed and the filed stamp clearly on them, but . . .

She had promised Luke ten dates.

What in the fuck had she been thinking?

She was Rebecca Darden, supposedly an intelligent lawyer. And she'd been manipulated by her ex-husband.

Husband.

Yeah, yeah. A technicality.

But why had she agreed to those terms in the first place? It wasn't like her to agree to anything that might put her at a disadvantage.

So . . . why?

Why agree to the kiss-slash-no feely-slash-ten dates plan?

Oh yeah, because she'd been overconfident and thought she could control herself around Luke. Which was a fucking joke since he'd *always* been able to make her melt. But she also couldn't deny—and dammit she really hated admitting this, even to herself—that she'd wanted to see if he *could* actually make her feel something.

And he had.

Oh boy, he had.

Her thighs clenched just remembering.

She sighed, picked up her cell, and leaned back in her chair, considering. It only took her a few minutes to face facts. She was in over her head, and that could only mean she had one recourse.

Bec needed to bring in the girls.

My apartment. Tonight at 7 pm. I'll provide wine.

A year ago, she never would have sent the text, but today, with her group of dirty best friends, she knew when she needed to call in reinforcements. They'd supported each other through thick and thin, and Bec *knew* they would have her back.

Abby replied first.

You okay?

Bec sent back:

Physically I'm fine. But I think I've just been put in an emotional blender.

Abby:

Damn. I can't believe someone got the best of Bec Darden, but I'm in and I'll bring something filled with a suitable amount of carbs.

Cecelia chimed in.

Colin and I are in Scotland. I'll conference in.

Then Rachel.

I'll bring my actual blender. I think this might call for more than wine.

Heather:

I'm in Berlin with Clay. I'll kick him out and be ready. A beat. Who do I need to kill?

Seraphina:

I'll bring something to soak up Rachel's booze.

After thanking her friends, Bec grinned and set down her cell. Her girls were the absolute best, and she didn't know what she would do without them.

Probably lose her mind, that was what.

But she couldn't shake the feeling that Luke might have already absconded with her brain.

Ten dates?

Fucking nuts.

THE DOORBELL RANG at a quarter to seven, and Bec hurried to answer it. She was still in her work clothes, having only made it home and inside a few minutes before.

"Hey," she said, swinging it open without looking through the peephole. "Come in. I'm—"

The words stuck in her throat.

Luke was outside her door. Again.

And he looked sexier than should be allowed in a pair of faded jeans, boots, and a fitted navy sweater.

"Hi," he said and pushed past her into the apartment, leaving her standing there, still holding the doorknob.

She let it go, grabbed his arm, and tried to shove him back out into the hall.

"I changed the code," she said. "I swear, I did."

He plucked her fingers from his biceps, clasped them in his. "You did." A shrug. "Turns out I'm good at picking your codes." He lifted her hand to his mouth, pressed a kiss to her knuckles. "Senior prom was a good night."

Her heart pulsed.

It had been.

And how in the hell had he remembered the date? Furthermore, how had he known she would use it?

"Don't think that was about you," she grumbled, tugging at their still-laced hands and trying to shepherd him out the door. "I was tired last night, and it was the first thing I thought of." She glared. "I have plans tonight. You need to leave."

Before her friends saw him.

That was a scene she really didn't want to deal with.

The verbal details would be bad enough. She didn't need to contend with the physical perfection of the specimen that was Luke.

"What kind of plans?"

His growly tone made her pause and narrow her eyes at him. "None of your fucking business, Pearson. We may still be married, but you don't have any right to know what I'm doing and when I'm doing it."

He cupped her cheek. "There's my Becky."

She jerked her head away. "*Bec.*"

"Bec," he repeated. "I won't mess up your plans. I only came to give you something and to get your number. I promised to call," he added at what was no doubt a confused expression on her face.

She hadn't been confused about the number part, rather the give her something part.

Was it a sexual reference?

Because, honestly, she wouldn't mind if Luke gave her *something* along those lines.

But then he held out his hand, and her heart skipped a beat.

On his palm sat a tiny glass dolphin.

She'd always loved dolphins. And chocolate for breakfast.

And he remembered.

Another tiny fissure appeared in that icy box deep in her heart, and panic promptly spiraled out from that point, spilling into her gut, making her hands shake. Luke seemed to realize this and carefully set the little dolphin on her console table then pulled out his phone.

"What's your number, sweetheart?"

Bec shook her head. This was too much, too soon. She was too vulnerable and couldn't risk . . . her heart, her happiness, *herself.*

"415-555-2345"

It wasn't Bec's voice that'd provided her cell number. She turned, saw that Abby, Rachel, and Seraphina were gathered in the hallway.

Abby flashed her a thumbs-up.

"Thank you, darlin'," Luke said. He started to leave, paused next to Bec. "I'll call you later."

And for the second time that day, she was at a loss for words.

"It's good to see you, Abigail."

Abby smiled beatifically up at him. "You, too, Luke." Then her eyes narrowed, and that smile faded. "You hurt her again, and I'll cut you." Rachel and Seraphina nodded in agreement.

Luke blinked. He'd lifted his arms as though to hug Abby, but froze mid-reach, eyeing the three women. "I won't," he promised solemnly.

Bec snorted. Yes, it was laced with derisiveness.

No, she didn't care.

Abby glanced at her. "Time to go, Luke."

He slanted one more look at Bec, and she didn't have to be smart or a lawyer or the top of her class to see it was filled with promise. She only needed to be a woman, to be *Luke's* woman.

Luke Pearson was back.

And he wouldn't be leaving any time soon.

SIX

Luke

HE'D JUST SAT in the driver's seat of his rental car when his phone buzzed. Considering he'd just sent a text to Bec, he assumed it would be a retort that would make his ears bleed.

The thought made him grin.

Then he opened the message.

That grin faded and his stomach twisted, because contrary to what he'd hoped, the message wasn't from his Becky, but rather from his mother.

I've given you a lot of rope, Luke.
I won't let you hang yourself with it.
-Mom

A man takes *one* leave of absence from the company he devoted a good portion of his adult life to, and everybody freaks out.

I'm fine, Mom. Enjoy your time in the Maldives.
Love you.

The " . . . " appeared on his screen, signaling a forthcoming reply, and Luke closed his eyes, praying for patience. His mom was not what one would call tech savvy—for one, she still signed her messages 'Mom'—and he knew that any message he received would be a long time coming as she typed out one . . . letter . . . at . . . a . . . time.

Sure enough, it took a solid two minutes for her to send:

You haven't been yourself since your engagement ended.

Of course, he hadn't. One moment he'd been prepared to walk down the aisle, to marry a woman he thought he loved, and the next, his life had taken a sharp right. Luke had been relieved —knees shaking, hands trembling, heart pounding relieved—that they couldn't pull the license. He'd known then he couldn't marry Tiffani. That she deserved better, more than an asshole like him.

And Luke realized how much of a fucking idiot he'd been all those years before. He'd lived in blissful ignorance for a long fucking time, pretending his marriage imploding had been Becky's fault—she'd filed the papers after all—but then he'd realized they were still married and . . . he'd allowed himself to remember everything.

How good it had been between them. How bad it had been at the end. What she'd done. What *he'd* done.

And, newsflash, his behavior had been appalling.

He'd held the thing he loved the most about Bec against her, had been jealous of her drive, of the career she was trying to build, of the early success she'd found when he'd been stuck with only two options: a shitty position, looking forward to years of paying his dues or caving and going to work for his father.

He hadn't caved, but he'd ended up in the family business anyway.

And before that? Luke had done everything in his power to push Becky away.

Not surprisingly, he'd succeeded.

I'm trying to change that, Mom. California is good for me.

He'd started the car and pulled out of the parking garage before his mom's reply came.

Change things faster. The business won't hold forever.

Yeah. *That* Luke knew firsthand.

Sighing, he drove to his hotel, back to the empty suite, to his laptop filled with emails about business concerns he wasn't supposed to be tackling during his time away, back to emails he was answering anyway.

What else did he have to do?

His life was empty, and the one woman he'd truly loved in his life didn't want anything to do with him.

Rightfully so, but . . . he was still bordering on pathetic.

Sighing, he dialed his COO, Brian, and went over a few of the more problematic issues, before promising to fly back to Texas for an important meeting the following week.

After they'd dealt with the pressing business concerns, Luke mentioned an idea that had been bouncing around in his brain since he'd come to California. Brian was a flat sort of guy, limited emotions, few words, and so Luke took his, "We should definitely explore that further," as a raring endorsement.

Hell, the other man had even included an adverb, and that *never* happened.

"Do me a favor," Luke said before he hung up, "pass along the grapevine that I'm working while here, okay?"

There was a pause then, "Your mother?"

"My mother," Luke agreed. "Help me put her at ease."

"Done."

Then the call disconnected and . . . silence.

Luke was alone again, but that had been a common enough occurrence over the years, and so he was used to it.

He clicked on the TV, called room service and ordered a hamburger, fries, and, what the hell, he added a slice of chocolate cake.

Luke Pearson sure knew how to live.

SEVEN

Bec

ABBY CLOSED the door and leaned back against it, staring at her with a glare that rivaled Bec's own signature Darden Death Glare.

"Put that away," Bec snapped, waving a hand through the air and turning toward the kitchen. "I'm going to spill everything, okay? That's why I called this emergency meeting for the Sextant."

Rachel followed her. "I'll grab the glasses."

"Thanks," Bec muttered, deliberately avoiding Seraphina and Abby's gazes. "Sit down and get the other two knuckleheads on the phone."

Sera stepped in front of her, arms crossed. "Why was Luke Pearson lurking in your hallway?"

"Living room!" Bec pointed.

Abby held up her cell, revealing CeCe and Heather's faces on the screen. "We're all here, so spill."

Bec grabbed a bottle and opener. "I need more wine for this."

Rachel snatched it from her. "Go, sit down. I'll do this."

"You don't know where everything is. I can—"

"*Bec.*"

A unison of voices calling her on her shit.

"Ugh. *Fine.*" She strode into the living room and plunked down onto the couch.

"Nope," Abby told her, tugging her back up and shoving her in the direction of her bedroom. "Pajamas first. We'll get everything ready."

Bec nodded and escaped to her bedroom.

Why had she invited this maelstrom of femininity into her house in the first place? Oh yeah, because she'd been trying to prove to herself that Luke's words from the past didn't matter . . . or not that they didn't matter so much as they were no longer true.

She wasn't just work, only work, all work. She wasn't a lawyer robot without a heart.

She was a living, breathing human with real feelings and emotions.

And like only seventy-five percent work.

Twenty-five, yup a solid twenty-five percent, were meaningful, important, and dare she say, significant sentiments because they did not revolve around her work.

Bec was just nodding to herself in the mirror, a confident, encouraging bob of her head she'd given herself more than once before an important case, when she heard the blender start up. And now that she was paying attention, she could also smell pizza. Or at least something equally carby and cheese-filled.

Her stomach growled as she slipped on a pair of pink fuzzy socks.

"Pizza's here!" Sera called just as Bec was pushing to her feet.

"*Yes.*" She opened the door and went out to join the girls.

Her shoulders inched higher and tighter with each step, but she forced herself to relax them. Even putting her desire to prove Luke wrong aside, she knew that calling in her friends was the right thing to do. They were there for each other, hands down, no holds barred, no judgment—okay, so maybe a *little* judgment because they truly wanted what was best for each other, and sometimes that required tough love with a dash of judgment thrown in.

Regardless, she'd handled Luke alone before, and look where that had gotten her.

She needed the Sextant, and she needed them STAT.

Rachel stuck a margarita in her hand the moment Bec crossed the threshold into the living room. "Drink first. Talk second."

Abby scoffed. "I disagree with that notion because . . . uh . . ." Her words trailed off, probably because Bec had drained the entire glass in just a few swallows. "Never mind."

Sera laced her arm through Bec's and led her to the couch. "So, Luke's in town, huh?"

Bec nodded, reaching for another glass, wine this time. Maybe the combo of the two liquors would bring her oblivion, make her forget that she'd agreed to go on ten dates with Luke. Maybe then she could pretend she hadn't been bested by the man who'd broken her heart.

"So who is Luke exactly?" Rachel asked.

"Bec's ex-boyfriend and fiancé. Sera, Bec, and I met him when we were all shipped off to boarding school," Abby said. "He went to the boys' high school next door."

"You had a *boyfriend?*" CeCe asked.

Bec bristled at the shock in her friend's tone. "I'm not asexual," she grumbled. "I've dated, had boyfriends." She gulped down some wine. "And, I like penises. I just haven't had much use for them of late."

"Sleeping with people isn't exactly dating." Sera grinned. "Also, I think the proper term is peni."

"Nope." Heather. "Definitely not. Also, *ew*, Sera. The word *peni* should never come out of your mouth."

"Why?" Sera made a face. "Why do you all get to be dirty and I can't even say *peni*?"

"It's penises!" Rachel said, lifting her own glass to her lips. "And I don't know, Sera. You're like . . . too innocent."

Blue eyes glared. "I own five vibrators!"

Silence then a collective, "*Ew*."

"Oh my God," Sera muttered. "You guys are evil."

"It's like an innocent old lady telling me how she likes to get off." Heather shuddered.

Sera glared. "I'm neither old nor innocent."

"You don't even like to curse," Bec reminded her.

"Well, how about this? Fuck. Fuckity. Fuck."

More silence.

Then Abby shook her head and wove her arm through Sera's. "Nope. Just doesn't compute. You're too nice, Sera."

"I've decided that being nice sucks," she muttered. "But"— she sighed and straightened her shoulders—"enough about my *innocence*. I want to hear more about Bec and Luke."

One big gulp of wine to fortify herself before Bec blurted, "We're married."

Silence. And this time it had nothing to do with Sera's vibrators.

Heather was the first to regain her voice. "Well, this is unexpected."

CeCe snorted. "Because she took a page out of your book?"

Heather shushed her. But CeCe's teasing was on point. Heather and her husband Clay had pulled a Vegas cliché by getting blackout drunk and then standing up before an Elvis impersonator to exchange vows.

Enemies in the business world to husband and wife, all before they'd gone on a single date.

"I didn't take a page out of Heather's book," Bec said, setting her glass down and leaning back against the couch. A pleasant swirling feeling was circling around in her head. "We did have a secret, impulsive wedding. It was just ten years ago."

And more silence.

"I—" Abby started to speak then stopped with a shake of her head, out of words for maybe the first time ever.

Sera touched Bec's arm. "Why didn't you tell us?"

She kept her eyes closed. "I thought we were divorced."

"There's a plot twist I didn't expect," Rachel said into the quiet.

Bec sighed. "We got married right before I graduated from law school. We'd been dating for a lot longer than that, though. Since senior year of high school." A shrug. "Getting married seemed like the next logical thing to do."

Abby found her words. "But we all expected you two to get married. You were together for ages. Why hide it?"

"His parents wanted us to wait. No." She shook her head, enjoying the way her brain seemed to slosh around in her skull. "That's not entirely true. Yes, they thought we were still a little young, but there were plenty of people in our circle who'd gotten hitched." A shrug. "Luke and I had always planned to get married. I guess I pushed the secret wedding because I wanted something that was ours and ours alone."

"Then what happened?" A gentle probe from Sera.

Bec smiled. "We had a really good nine months. We'd graduated, were both working, living together. It was—" A sigh, her eyes filling with tears at the memory of late nights pouring over work, ordering in pizza, getting up early to brew his favorite type of coffee, making love, and Luke holding her tightly afterward. "It was about as perfect as you could get."

"Is he hot?" Heather.

Four sets of eyes—three in Bec's living room, one through the airwaves—swiveled to glare at Heather.

"*Really?*" Sera asked.

But Bec shot Heather a grateful look, which Heather acknowledged with a nod. She might be opening up to her friends, might be sharing her sad, sad tale, but dammit, she wasn't a fucking watering pot, and she absolutely refused to cry over Luke Pearson.

Been there, done that. Got the souvenir shot glass.

"He's even hotter now," she admitted, begrudgingly.

"I second that," Rachel chimed in. "Well, I didn't know him before, but the view I got tonight . . ." She brought her fingers to her mouth, affecting an Italian chef. "Muah! The man can fill out a pair of jeans."

Abby sank down on the couch next to Bec. "Yes, he's hot, but what's he doing here now?"

Bec explained about his engagement, the courthouse burning down, and their divorce paperwork not going through.

"Is he still engaged?" CeCe asked, concern edging into her voice.

Bec froze. "I don't know."

Heather and Abby began talking, Rachel and CeCe chiming in with an occasional comment, but Sera didn't join the conversation. Instead, she snatched up Bec's phone, smiled at what she saw on the screen then began typing something, thumbs moving furiously.

"What are you—?"

"He's not engaged," Sera announced.

The girls stopped talking.

"How do you know?" Heather asked.

Sera shrugged. "I asked him, and he said, and I quote 'I couldn't marry Tiffani because I knew I was still in love with

Becky.'" She held the phone to her chest. "Aw. That's so sweet."

Meanwhile, Bec couldn't find a retort because her heart was pounding.

I was still in love with Becky.

Love.

Becky.

Finally, her brain unstuck. "Give me that," she said, snatching it from Sera's hands.

It's Bec.

A pause.

Hi, sugar pie.

She narrowed her eyes at the phone, damned stubborn man.

Bec. Not Becky. And sure as shit not sugar pie.

Barely a heartbeat before,

How about sweetheart?

"Oh, I *like* him," Rachel said, making Bec jump and look up from her cell. She hadn't realized that Abby, Sera, and Rachel were huddled around her.

"What'd he say?" Heather asked.

"She said her name is Bec, just Bec, and so then he asked if he could call her sweetheart," Abby stage-whispered.

Bec made a sound of disgust when she saw Heather grin.

"You guys are the worst."

"You love us," CeCe said, lips curved into a wide smile.

"Maybe," Bec grumbled.

"Group hug!" Abby declared, and before Bec could protest or wiggle away, three sets of arms wrapped around her.

"I'm hugging you, too," CeCe declared.

"I'm not," Heather declared. "This is just too cheeseball for words."

"Shut it," Abby said. "You love our hugs."

Heather sniffed but didn't deny that fact.

Bec's phone buzzed, and they pulled back, all looking at the screen. On it was a day and time, followed by a question mark.

They all glanced at Bec for an explanation. "I kissed him—"

Sera squealed.

"To prove I didn't feel anything for him."

If Bec had been feeling amused, she might have laughed at the way her friend's face fell.

"We made a bet," she said. "If I felt nothing, he'd go away and we'd officially get divorced."

"And if you felt something?" Heather asked.

"I'd go on ten dates with him. One for every year we've spent apart."

Sera sighed. "That's so romantic."

"And?" Abby prompted. "What happened?"

Bec made a face in answer.

"Holy shit," Rachel said.

CeCe crowed. "This man must be something to get the best of Rebecca Fucking Darden."

"Don't remind me," Bec muttered. "I made a shitty agreement, and I felt something, and now I've got to go on ten dates with the only guy who's ever broken my heart."

"But—"

"He couldn't handle me or my success a decade ago. How the fuck is he going to react differently today? My work—"

"Doesn't define you," Heather said.

If anyone besides Heather had said those words, Bec would have been able to brush them aside. But coming from Heather O'Keith, quite possibly the only other person on the planet who'd pulled as many hours as her, they weren't so easy to dismiss.

"Yeah," she muttered.

"I think the bigger question here," Abby said, "is why did you agree to the deal in the first place?"

"I—"

Abby made a slashing motion with her hand. "No. No excuses about how Luke is so sexy he made you lose your head. That's bullshit." She met Bec's stare head on. "And you know it. *No one* has ever made you do something you didn't want to, so you need to come to terms with why you agreed to this in the first place." She touched Bec's hand. "And whether your agreement means that deep down you really want this second chance with Luke."

"Damn," Rachel said, tone awe-filled. "She's good."

Sera smiled. "Yes, she is."

Bec didn't reply. She'd been too shocked to the core by the truth in Abby's words.

Thankfully, her friends seemed to recognize that, so they changed the subject to CeCe and Colin's latest travels, and then a hilarious story involving Abby's son Hunter, and then an idiotic investor who'd tried to double-cross Heather and hadn't stood a chance.

A few hours later, Heather and CeCe hung up, and Rachel, Sera, and Abby packed their things.

Hugs and goodbyes and a raised eyebrow glance from Abby punctuated their departure. Bec nodded, letting her friend know she'd truly heard her statement earlier that evening and was seriously considering it. There were some things that didn't require words after close to twenty years of friendship, and Bec's acknowledgment of Abby's insight was one of those.

With one last goodbye, she closed and locked her door.

Her cell buzzed and she wasn't surprised to see a text from Abby. Yes, there were some things that didn't require speaking, but her friend didn't often have the willpower to be silent.

Go along for the ride. You might decide you like it.

Bec sighed, sent a text back,

I did that once. Want to guess where it got me?

A beat then another buzz.

Multiple orgasms?

Yes, but that was beside the point.

Goodnight, Abs.

One more buzz.

Goodnight.

A beat. Then a GIF of a cheerleader shouting, "Go for it!" came through. Bec grinned despite herself and headed into her bedroom. Her friends had done the dishes, despite her protests, but it *was* nice to just slip between the cool cotton sheets and close her eyes.

Unfortunately, they didn't stay closed for long.

Maybe it was the alcohol. Maybe it was Abby's words. Maybe she'd just gone insane.

Or perhaps it was all of the above.

Because Bec opened the text chain from Luke, grinning when she noticed that Sera had saved his number with the name Sir Sexy Pants.

The man sure could fill out a pair of Levi's.

Not the point, but her slightly-buzzed mind still spent a good minute picturing that yummy, two-glorious-handfuls of an ass in those faded jeans.

Yup. She wouldn't mind grabbing on to that as he pounded into her—

Focus.

Bec blinked. Read back through the chain and mentally lifted her chin as she typed out a response.

Sweetheart TBD. Depends on how good you are on Friday night.

A long minute passed before a reply came through.

I mean to prove to you how good I can be.

Heaven help her, but she wanted to see exactly how good that was.

EIGHT

Luke

UNACCOUNTABLY NERVOUS, that was Luke.

And not only because he wasn't sure if Becky would show up for their first date, but also because . . . he wasn't sure if Becky would show up for their date.

Hilarious.

But bad dad jokes aside, Luke had a sudden case of what-if-he-was-doing the wrong thing? Not about coming back for Becky or trying to convince her that they were worth a second chance . . . but what if at the end of this she didn't want to be with him?

Then it was too late for doubts.

A car pulled into the empty lot and parked right next to his rental. He knew it was Becky even before he caught a glimpse of her through the windshield. The car just screamed Rebecca Darden, sleek and dark with just enough of an edge to make him proceed with caution.

Luke pushed off the hood of his rental, made his way over to

Becky's, but before he could open the door and help her to her feet, she'd gotten out.

That hadn't changed.

Still independent, still would force him to find creative ways to care for her.

"Hi, sweetheart."

She crossed her arms. "Don't sweetheart me," she said. "You haven't earned *sweetheart* privileges yet."

He swept in, pressed a quick kiss to her cheek. It took every bit of his willpower to not stay close, to not soak in her scent and nuzzle the spot just beneath her jaw that used to drive her crazy. The only reason Luke didn't do those things—well, two reasons he supposed—was because, first, she hadn't given him those rights and, second, she was wary. This would be a battle won with patience and small steps.

And if Luke had learned nothing else over the years, it was how to be patient.

Patient while he paid his dues in the corporate world. Patient while he helped a father who despised needing him. Patient while he dealt with a nervous board and paranoid investors.

He could be patient if required.

His Becky required it.

"Hi," he repeated, stepping so close that she had to tilt her head back in order to keep meeting his gaze. That nearness fucked with his mind, made him want to get closer, to bend and close the gap between their mouths. But only millimeters separating them also meant he could see Becky's reaction. See he wasn't the only one affected.

And that gave him hope in his plan.

Her lips parted, tongue darting out to moisten the bottom one. Just that tiny poke of pink against red had him hardening.

He wanted that tongue in his mouth. He wanted that tongue on his cock.

He wanted *his* tongue in—

Not. The. Time.

Luke sucked in a breath and took a step back. "Come on." He turned, walked away from her, even though that was the last damn thing he wanted to do.

But *patience*.

Stifling a sigh, Luke moved to the edge of the parking lot, to where he'd set everything up, pretending casualness but not actually relaxing until he heard Becky's soft footsteps trail him across the asphalt.

"What are we doing here—?" Drawing equal with him, she sucked in a breath.

"Remember senior prom?"

Becky had gone stag, even though they'd been dating, wanting to support Abby and Sera, who'd broken up with their boyfriends just before the dance, and Luke had spent the whole night drooling over her in her skintight red dress.

But it had been after the dance was over, when she'd climbed into his car and they'd driven away from the school together, that they'd created the real memories.

He laced his fingers through hers, tugging her forward and onto the plaid blanket he'd laid out. A bottle of sparkling apple cider sat in one corner, sandwiched by two glasses, and a box of It's-Its sat in the other. Vanilla ice cream sandwiched between two oatmeal cookies and dipped in chocolate, they were a treat from Becky's childhood.

Luke had been eighteen, okay? It's-Its and sparkling cider were about as romantic as he'd gotten at that age.

Hence the blanket on the grass in an empty park. Yes, the night had been pretty, the stars as bright then as they were that evening, but he hadn't considered much besides getting Becky alone and convincing her to let him score a kiss . . . or more.

Eighteen, remember?

Her eyes hit on the box of treats and her lips curved. "Really?"

He shrugged. "It was the first time you let me kiss you, of course, I had to reenact it."

"Kissing is what got us into this mess in the first place, remember?" she grumbled, but she slipped her hand from his and sank down onto the blanket anyway, reaching for the box of treats. "A little easier to get these this time," she said.

Considering Luke had gone to close to a dozen stores back then trying to find Becky's official Bay Area It's-Its—no East Coast imposters would do—he had to agree.

Today, he'd visited one grocery store and scored the goods. Selecting a park that had been similar to theirs from that night had been a little more difficult. Turned out that creeping around neighborhood parks after dark made him look like a drug dealer, at least according to the cops who'd visited him while he was scoping one out a few nights before.

Luckily, handcuffs hadn't been involved . . . or rather, Luke hadn't ended up *wearing* them. Thankfully, the officers had taken pity on him after he'd confessed all, even giving him a hint for a good location to take her.

Not that Becky needed to know any of that, especially the almost-handcuffed part. Tonight, he just wanted her to relax, to remember the good things about them.

Or at least that Luke knew her well enough to bring her It's-Its.

She tore into the box, pulled one out. He sat next to her, waiting while she unwrapped it and devoured half. Only after she sighed contentedly, pausing her scarfing for a few moments, did Luke ask, "As good as you remember?"

Becky turned her face toward his, and he saw a hint of the girl she'd been.

Content to just sit with him, to enjoy a grocery store treat, to smile up at him like he was the answer to everything wrong in her life, in the world.

A hero because he'd bought her some chocolate-covered, ice cream-filled oatmeal cookies that had been half-melted by the time they'd eaten them, despite the cooler he'd packed them in.

Life was simpler in high school.

"I haven't had one of these in ages," she murmured. "Still the best ever."

He opened the cider, poured two glasses, and handed her one. "Still a good way to stave off homesickness?"

Becky took the glass and sipped before setting it aside. She lay back on the blanket, arms crossed behind her head, gaze on the stars. "I'm home now."

"Doesn't mean there isn't something to miss."

"Hmm." She kept her eyes on the sky. "Stop hovering over me and lie down. The stars are beautiful."

"*You're* beautiful."

"Pish." Becky waved a lazy hand. "Down."

Luke complied, lying back on the blanket, careful to keep a few inches between them, just like he'd done as a scared teenager, trying to make a good impression on the girl he was infatuated with.

He was still striving for that good impression.

Or at least a reformed one.

They stared up at the sky, silence descending between them, not uncomfortable, exactly, but filled with the tension of the past and the high stakes of the present.

"I'd half-expected you not to show up," he said after a few minutes.

Becky shrugged. "I made a promise."

"Why *did* you make the promise?" he asked, rolling to his side to study her. Moonlight gilded the lines of her face—turning her pert nose, smooth jaw, and plump lips into something reminiscent of a marble statue.

Beautiful and yet somehow untouchable.

She shifted onto her side and watched him, gray eyes almost black in the dim light. "You won the bet, remember?"

He raised a brow, waited, and . . . there it was.

The slightest flicker of emotion. She wasn't just holding up her side of the agreement, there was something more, a deeper feeling, a draw that wasn't easy for her to dismiss, and for now, that was enough.

"I had wet dreams about that red dress of yours for years." Luke had gotten his sign, and now he wanted to say something to jar her out of her worries, to see the woman who didn't take any shit, to see that sass he loved so much.

The teasing statement worked. Becky's jaw dropped open, and fire flashed in her eyes. "You're a pig."

"You knew that I was slavering over you that whole night, watching you dance with the girls, hiding a boner in my slacks, and dying to get my hands on you."

A wicked smile curved her lips. "Maybe I liked teasing you."

"All I knew is that I *loved* it." He laughed. "Spank bank material for days."

"Such. A. Pig."

"Definitely the luckiest pig around," he said.

"You were the sweetest boy around." She sighed, expression almost gentle. "I think that night—the treats on a moon-gilded blanket—was the first time in my life someone did something for me just because they knew I'd enjoy it."

And he'd ruined that. *Fuck.*

He gritted his teeth against the fury he felt at being such an idiot. "You deserved the world, and I—"

Soft fingers brushed his jaw. "You always were good at beating yourself up." She rolled back over, eyes up on the stars again. "You know what I remember from that night?"

He shook his head when her head tilted back toward him, her stare finding his.

"I remember you being upset at yourself that you'd forgotten to bring an extra blanket because I got cold in my skimpy dress. I remember you giving me your jacket and the first glass of cider. I remember the feel of your lips on mine, the heat of your tongue, the way our mouths seemed to fit perfectly together." Her voice dropped. "And . . . I remember thinking it was the best first kiss a girl could ask for."

"I—"

"The problem between us never was chemistry or romance. And it wasn't grand gestures or simple date nights. You were always way better at that stuff than I was."

He was still spinning from her revelation that he'd been her first kiss. She'd never told him that, and Luke felt a pulse of disquiet, wondering what else she might have withheld. He brushed the back of his knuckles down her arm. "So if that wasn't the issue, then what *was* our problem?"

"We weren't compatible," she said, tone less matter of fact than he'd expected, considering the plain words. In fact, it was almost gentle, at least until she pushed to her feet. "We wanted different things. We *still* want different things. Simple as that."

Luke sat up, but she sidestepped him when he reached for her hand then bent to pick up the box of It's-Its and turned in the direction of her car.

"I want you," he said. "Any or every part you want to give me."

She paused, fingers on the door handle. "What happens when you don't like what you're given?"

"That's not possible—"

Her chin dropped to her chest. "Nothing was ever enough for you, Luke. Not me. Not us. Not—"

"*You're* enough."

Wrong answer. Becky shook her head, pulled open the door, and got into her car. Luke watched her drive away, not sure if he'd blown this whole thing before it even got off the ground or if progress had been made.

The past still had its claws in them.

The plus was that Becky was actually talking to him.

NINE

Bec

SHE WAS RAW INSIDE.

She had to take back control.

She . . . needed to focus on work.

Bec sighed and pushed her chair back. It was Monday morning, and normally she would be raring to start her work week, but . . . It's-Its and a plaid blanket, memories of tentative kisses and strong arms.

Luke Pearson had been back in her life for less than a week, and last night he'd—

What?

Made her feel something? Made her ache for their past to have been different?

Of course. But fuck, the thing about life was that they *couldn't* go back.

And so now she was scrambling, trying to find her happy in the law and loopholes and briefs, and she still couldn't change the past.

She and Luke had their chance, and it was ridiculous to try to resurrect something that had nearly destroyed them both.

Stupid, even.

Rebecca Darden wasn't stupid.

She had to end this. Now. Yesterday.

Picking up her cell, Bec began composing the text in her mind. She'd have to be firm, deliberate in pushing him away, otherwise—

Her eyes processed what was on the screen.

She hadn't even heard her phone buzz, but sure enough, on the screen was a text from Luke.

You promised me ten dates, don't back out now.

"Ugh!" She flopped back into her chair, temper spiking. If the annoying specimen of a man had gone sweet and gentle, tried to convince her to keep giving him another chance nicely, it would have been so easy to give him the kiss-off. But, dammit, he'd gone and called her honor into question.

Well, fuck honor.

She opened the text chain, started to type a reply, but another message came through.

Don't be a chicken now, Darden.

Double ugh. Now he was questioning her lady balls.

And, double dammit, she had giant lady balls. Luke Pearson didn't scare her.

Nope. Not in the least.

Then why are you looking for one of those loopholes you're so good at finding? Hmm? her brain accused.

Nine dates. Nine nights. Nine—

Oh God, she couldn't do this. Any good attorney worth her

salt knew when she needed to take a step back and regroup. She groaned, dropped her head to her desk. Because how did she regroup against the yumminess that was Luke?

Yumminess?

Had she really just used that word?

Thunk. Maybe she could use her desk to knock some sense back into her brain. *Thunk. Thunk. Th—*

"I knew you'd be like this."

Bec glanced up and saw Seraphina standing in the doorway of her office.

"What is it with everyone invading my work lately?"

Sera propped one hand on her hip, her *asset*s jiggling with the movement. Really, her boobs were insane. If Bec hadn't seen them appear junior year, she would have been convinced her friend had spawned from another planet. Slender, a beautiful face, and as tall as Bec, Sera was beyond buxom and even more gorgeous than most actresses or models.

And the worst part about it?

She was *nice.*

Like, super nice. Like as nice and kind and beautiful on the inside as she was on the out.

Great. Now Bec sounded like a teenage Valley Girl.

Like this. Like that. Like—

"Why are you staring at me like I've suddenly sprouted antennae?"

"Because your boobs are superhuman."

Seraphina rolled her eyes, crossed to the front of Bec's desk, and all but threw a container of food at her. And no wonder Bec hadn't heard her phone buzz. Despite feeling off her game, she'd worked almost six hours straight.

"Molly's?" she asked hopefully.

Sera scoffed. "As if I'd bring you anything else." She dropped into the chair and opened her own container.

"Spinach, goat cheese, and apples. Plus, I got you extra walnuts."

"You're a goddess."

Sera huffed. "That's what the idiot cashier said."

Seraphina wasn't unaware that she was beautiful. She'd spent a lifetime dealing with boys and men, *and* women for that matter, fawning over her. But Sera was also the least superficial person Bec had ever met.

Many a person had said that Sera's beauty was wasted on her because she just didn't care about the way she looked.

She didn't want to be an actress or a model or an influencer.

She wanted to find Mr. Right and settle down and be a mom.

Unfortunately, all the potential Mr. Rights seemed to be blinded by her beauty. They discounted her smarts—she was a successful real estate agent—and treated her like the dumb blonde bimbo she wasn't.

"Men are idiots."

"Not all of them," Sera said through a mouthful of spinach. "Some of them are good."

Forever optimistic.

"Don't look at me," Sera added. "I know I'm naïve, but I can't help it if I'm holding out for my happily ever after. Abby, CeCe, Heather, Rachel, they've all found someone. We can, too."

Bec made a noise that could be interpreted as agreement . . . or disagreement. One of those two, for sure.

Sera pushed the container closer Bec and continued to eat. Bec stared suspiciously at her friend, waiting for the interrogation to start. She wouldn't break under Sera's probing—she was Rebecca *Fucking* Darden, after all—but she also wasn't looking forward to an argument.

When Sera got an idea in her head, she resembled a dog to a bone.

But despite Bec opening the salad and taking a large bite—fucking delicious with the extra candied walnuts, by the way—Sera's inquisition didn't come.

They ate their salads in between Sera relating the persistent pickup attempts of the cashier at Molly's, and pretty soon her friend had her in hysterics over the much younger man's melodrama.

"I mean, I try not to be judgmental. Age is really just a number, but I'm not into college drama students and especially one who can break into a soliloquy from *Romeo and Juliet* at the drop of a hat when I politely turn him down." She raised her fork toward the ceiling, punctuating her statement. "Does he even know how that play ends? This just in: it's a freaking tragedy."

"Unbelievable," Bec said.

"The worst part?" Sera moaned. "My love life's the real tragedy."

"That's not true," Bec felt obliged to say, though if she was being truly honest, tragedy *was* a fitting word for the gorgeous inside and out Sera to have not found a man to really appreciate her.

Sera dropped her container into the trash. "It's true. *Very* true. But then again, I'm not the one who has a sexy Texan wanting a second chance with her."

There it was.

Bec sighed. "Sera—"

She lifted her hands in surrender. "I'm not going to say anything, but if *I* had a man in my life who looked at me the way Luke Pearson looks at you . . ."

"That's saying *something*."

Sera kept talking. "Further that, Luke gets under your skin,

Bec. He always has, and for a woman like you, that's critical. Otherwise, it's just too easy for you to ignore the men you date."

"I don't ignore men!"

"Scott, Steven, Sam, Sean, Michael." Sera ticked off the names on her fingers. "Also, sidenote, you date too many men whose names start with the letter S." A grin. "I think it's the perfect time to include one that begins with L. Maybe even a boyfriend"—she coughed—"or a *husband* that beings with L."

Bec lifted one brow, disregarding the L assertion and restating the important facts. "I do *not* ignore men."

Sera did some disregarding of her own. "Luke is who you're supposed to be with, don't you see? He's your chance at an HEA! It's the perfect trope—a second chance romance with your high school sweetheart."

"Sera." Bec sighed, rubbed her temples. "Things aren't that simple. Real life isn't fiction."

"I know that."

"Except, you don't. You're so sweet and innocent, and you believe that everyone has good inside of them." Bec tossed her own container into the trash. "But I've seen shit. The world isn't good. There are loads of people who don't have your best interests in mind, who don't have any qualms about breaking your heart when you give them all the pieces of yourself."

Sera leaned back in her chair. "Ah."

Bec had been ready and raring for a monologue. Sera's *ah* took the wind out of her sails. "*Ah*, what?"

"You're scared."

Now *that* was just enough. That was the second time in the span of an hour that someone had accused her of being scared. She was Bec Darden, scared wasn't in her vernacular—unless it was felt by the person on the receiving end of her death stare.

"I'm not scared," Bec said. "I'm not the one who keeps

putting my life on hold, waiting for someone who may never come. I'm living and—"

Sera stood. "I'm going to stop you right there."

Bec blinked at Sera's tone. Never, and she meant *never*, had she heard such a tone from her friend's mouth. It was sharp and reprimanding and made Bec feel about two inches tall.

"I may be stupid for holding on to hope that someday someone may love me for the person who I am inside. That may be a *fucking* pipe dream"—Bec blinked again. Sera and F-bombs rarely mixed—"but at least I'm not too scared to take a chance on something just because it might make me vulnerable. And I think that makes me the brave one of this pair, don't you?"

She strode to the door, paused with her fingers on the handle. "Also, nice try on the pushing people away thing. It's kind of your specialty."

A heartbeat later, Sera was gone, the door closing softly behind her.

Bec would have much preferred a slam.

But then again, if Sera *had* slammed the door, it would have confirmed to Bec that her friend was irrational and emotional rather than logical and smart and . . . maybe right.

So, in full Sera-rant-hangover mode, she texted Luke. Just to prove to herself that Sera *was* wrong and Bec wasn't scared or unsure or—

Shut. Up.

It didn't matter why. Only that she did text Luke and found herself committing to a date the following evening.

Name your time and place, Pearson. Only nine more dates until you're out of my life forever.

TEN

Luke

WHY HAD he decided it was a good idea to give his woman a weapon?

His Becky stared at him, weighing the ax in the palm of her hand. Then her eyes dropped to his groin, and Luke had to resist the urge to wince and cup his dick protectively.

Her lips twitched, and she turned to face the target, throwing the ax in a near perfect arch. It hit the bull's-eye but didn't stick, falling to the floor with a clatter.

"Nice," he said, picking up his own ax without any of Becky's unspoken threats.

"Come on, Mountain Man," she teased. "Show me how to work that hard, *hard* blade."

Considering he was mid-release when she said that, Luke was unsurprised that his ax missed the target completely and crashed to the floor. "Sexual euphemisms?" he asked, lifting one brow. "Really?"

A shrug, though her mouth was curved into a smirk. "If

we're revisiting our teenage and college years, then all of the *hard* puns fit, don't you think?"

"We never threw axes in high school," he said, walking over to pick his up from the floor.

"No," she said and hopped to sit on the little half-wall that formed the back of their booth. She was wearing skintight jeans and a plaid flannel with one too many of the buttons undone for his psyche.

Hell, who was he kidding?

They'd been together all of twenty minutes, and Luke had spent most of it fantasizing about what her reaction would be if he unbuttoned the rest of the fabric, spreading it wide, kissing down the soft expanse of her stomach, slipping his fingers under the waistband of her jeans—

"But we did go camping for our senior trip, which I'm sure you remember." One blonde brow lifted. "Considering it was the night we both lost our virginity."

Luke swallowed hard as he set the ax on the table.

Their boarding schools were technically separate—all boys in his, all girls in hers—but they'd combined for events like dances and the seniors' camping trip. So, yes, he'd been thinking of that weekend when he'd seen the ad for this place, of the outdoor games they'd played, of him pretending to help Becky with her archery skills—even though she'd been better than him by far.

It had been a weekend of teasing touches, of sneaking away for a few kisses, and yes, of their first time.

Luke crossed over to where she sat on the half-wall, nudging her legs apart so he could stand between them. Becky's smile was teasing, and he wanted to kiss it off her lips. Especially when that dangerous little pink tongue of hers darted out, wetting her bottom lip, and her eyes went hot. "I think you'd like my hard, *hard* blade," he told her, somehow managing to not crack up when he said it.

Probably because his *blade* was, as Becky had said, hard, *hard*.

"Yeah?" Teasing laced with heat in her tone and so fucking tempting.

He leaned in, close enough to smell the floral scent of her shampoo, to feel her hot breath against his lips. "Yeah," he said. "I'd make sure you enjoyed it. You know that."

"Yeah?" she said again and leaned even closer, only millimeters separating their mouths and, fuck it all, he couldn't help himself.

Luke kissed that pretty mouth.

Thank God, she kissed him back. Her arms came around his neck, her breasts pressed flush against his chest, and that pert little tongue slipped into his mouth.

One hand gripped her hip, tugging her snuggly against him, while the other wove into her hair—hanging down her back in gentle waves that were beyond fucking sexy. He tilted her head, angling their mouths in order to find that perfect fit.

And then he lost himself in his Becky, kissing her the way she loved, groaning when she rose pressed closer to him, memorizing those soft, breathy moans rising from the back of her throat.

Luke's hand was sliding down to the buttons of her shirt when he remembered himself, remembered they were in a very public place.

One more stroke of his tongue, one more nip on the corner of her mouth.

Then he forced himself to step back.

And promptly almost kissed her again.

Because her mouth was swollen and reddened, and her eyes

were glazed. Because she reached for him and the feel of her hands against his chest was every-*fucking*-thing.

Fuck, but what wouldn't he give to have her back in his hotel room.

Except . . . sex was never the issue between them. They could scorch the cotton sheets right off a bed. But sex wasn't the answer now. It was everything else that needed fixing.

So he carefully trapped Becky's hands then stepped back, putting enough distance between them that he was no longer tempted.

Or rather, *less* tempted.

"Your turn," he told her and shoved an ax into those palms.

Then considered himself lucky that she didn't cut off his hard, *hard* blade and instead slowly moved to the starting line and threw.

Bull's-eye.

He stared over at his Becky and knew he was in big, *big* trouble.

But it was trouble of the best damned kind.

"You know what I don't get?" Becky asked an hour later, as they sat at a nearby restaurant chowing down on quintessential bar food. She held a half-eaten French fry between her fingers and dipped it in a pile of ketchup on her plate—or rather, she used it as a vessel to get the maximum amount of ketchup into her mouth.

She might as well just drink it straight from the bottle.

"What?" he asked when she'd swallowed, reaching for his own fry and scooping up what he considered a reasonable amount of ketchup, though Becky had already teased him more than once about his "dainty dipping."

"Why come back now?"

A reasonable question.

Though one he'd avoided discussing with any depth because he didn't really have a great answer.

How could he explain something he didn't understand himself?

How could he explain the relentless urge to make things different between them, that Becky was the piece that had been missing in his life?

"And silence," she said, picking up her beer.

Luke was aware enough to sense the edge of hurt under the droll tone.

"It would have been easier to stay away," he told her. "To have my lawyer contact you and get officially divorced, to marry Tiffani and just move on."

Bec plunked the glass down on the table. "Wow."

He snagged her wrist when she would have turned away. "I'm not going to lie. I considered doing just that." His thumb brushed lightly against her skin. "But I knew I couldn't."

She yanked her arm free, signaled their waiter for the check. "Well, you should have saved yourself the trouble and stayed away."

"Becky," he began.

"It's. Bec." She leaned close and hissed, "It would have been better if you stayed away. Instead, you waltzed back into my life on your terms, demanding my attention, and disrupting every-thing. I was fine, dammit. Totally fine a-and—"

Luke froze, the slight hitch in her tone telling him more than anything else could.

She might be putting on a good front, but his Becky was rattled and, honestly, he couldn't blame her. He'd shown up out of nowhere and had spent the last two weeks pressing her buttons.

"I'm sorry."

"—And you don't get to—" She froze. "You're *what?*"

One corner of his mouth ticked up. "I know they're words I haven't said nearly often enough, but I'm sorry. I'm sorry I was such an ass then . . . *now.*" Her eyes softened, so he pressed on. "I'm sorry I didn't know what a good thing I had. I'm sorry I stormed back into your life without warning." He cupped her cheek. "But I'm not sorry that I'm trying to get you to give me a second chance. I spent the last decade searching for something, trying to prove myself to my bosses, my family, myself . . . and you want to know what I learned?"

A shrug.

"That the person I should have been proving myself to was you."

She shook her head. "Luke—"

"I had all this anger inside me—fury that my parents sent me away to school in the first place, that my father didn't think I was smart enough to succeed on my own and the only avenue my dumb ass had was the family business."

"You're not dumb, Pearson."

He scoffed. "You're brilliant, sweetheart. Always have been, and I was so *fucking* jealous of that, of how proud my parents were of your success. I was resentful when my father kept telling me that I should marry you because you were the best a fuck-up like me was going to get—"

"*What?*"

He released her hand, pushed his plate away. "When we moved away to school, he reinforced that. *Strongly.*" Luke forced down the old frustration. "After he reminded me that the only reason I got into business school at all was because he'd donated five million for the new tech building."

"That's—"

Her sentence was cut off when the waiter deposited their check.

Eyes deliberately not meeting hers, Luke reached for his wallet to pay. When he went to drop his credit card on the bill, she covered his hands with her own. "Luke."

He pulled back.

"Look at me."

Unable to deny her, he met her gaze.

She studied him for a long time, gray eyes penetrating. Then finally she nodded, as though she'd judged what he'd said as truth.

"Why didn't you tell me?"

A soft question. One with a shitty answer.

"I was a twenty-five-year-old man." A beat. "I was an idiot."

Her mouth curved up. "Well, that was a given."

"I'm not twenty-five anymore." Luke touched her cheek. "After you left, I started a company. It did well, and in the end, it was my Dad who needed me."

"I heard about Breeze"—the company he'd sold when he'd moved back to Pearson Energy—"it did a lot more than *well*."

He shrugged. "Its success had a lot less to do with me and a lot more to do with having been lucky enough to find the right people." Breeze focused on wind technology and their R&D department had revolutionized the way batteries stored extra power on windy days, partitioning it up so it could be used on days where the weather didn't cooperate. The process was now used in most wind farms throughout the world.

"You're being modest."

Luke grinned. "Another thing I've learned over the years."

"What happened with your father?"

The urge to immediately close down was intense, but Luke knew he couldn't do that anymore. He'd wounded Becky in the past by refusing to talk about things, by shutting her down when she did ask . . . and then being resentful when she played the role of a glutton for punishment and pushed harder.

"Without getting into all the gritty details," Luke said, "let's just say my father made some bad investments."

"Your tone makes it seem like he made a *lot* of bad investments."

He nodded. "Enough that Pearson Energy was six months from folding."

Becky gasped.

"I know. Breeze licensed technology and partnered with them until they were back in the black." He turned his palms up, laced their fingers together. "Dad never forgave me. That's the irony of it all. For once, I was the savior, the one who'd been smart enough to make a difference, and he resented me for it."

"Asshole."

He squeezed her hands. "I won't disagree with you." He sighed. "Especially because he made me running Pearson a contingency of my mom and sister receiving their inheritance. Not that he asked me to step in and help him with things while he was alive. I only found out at the reading that if I didn't step in as CEO, the estate would be donated to charity."

Becky's brows pulled together. "I'm not sure that was legal."

Luke smiled. "My lawyer didn't think so either, but I was worried about what a legal fight would do to my sister and mom, and Breeze was ready for a new direction. I'm still on the board, but the new president is incredibly brilliant."

She pulled one hand free, dunked another fry. "Why do you sound so . . ." She wrinkled her nose. "I mean, that's *a lot* for anyone to compartmentalize. How are you so normal?"

"Therapy."

Her eyebrows pulled down and together.

"I'm serious. *Actual* therapy. Well, that and five years of chasing my father's demons down the halls at Pearson. Therapy.

Hallways. Both of those things helped me come to terms with a lot of stuff." He grinned. "I'm semi-well-adjusted now."

"Semi, I think is the key word," Becky said, but she left her hand in his and then changed the subject to one of her latest cases, relating a funny tale about her intern freaking out because he'd spilled coffee on an important brief. ". . . I couldn't help it," she said. "I waited until he came back in with a blow dryer he'd procured from somewhere and started blasting the sheets to tell him that I had an electronic copy on the cloud."

Luke had shifted closer as she spoke, until their sides pressed together, until he could almost pretend this was a real date, one he hadn't tricked, cajoled, *forced* her to come on.

The only thing he held on to was that she didn't push him away.

Maybe there was hope yet.

ELEVEN

Bec

LUKE WASN'T OUT of her life.

Not at all.

He'd somehow talked her into letting him walk her back to her apartment, and even though she'd licked her lips and sidled close to him on the ride up, he hadn't kissed her. Just punched the code on her elevator—which she'd changed again after the last time they'd ridden up together and which he'd guessed . . . again.

Bec sighed. She really shouldn't have picked the day she'd passed the bar.

Especially when memories of that night swarmed her. Of Luke struggling to open a bottle of champagne, of them giggling as they sipped the frothy beverage. He'd also brought her a chocolate cake, and because their apartment was almost completely packed up, they'd searched through the filled boxes for plates and cups—only managing to find one plastic fork— then had taken turns feeding each other bites in between drinking straight from the bottle.

Such a different time. She'd been such a different woman.

So sweet.

Both the cake and Luke Pearson.

Not her. *Never* her.

But she couldn't deny that Luke had always managed to bring out a softness in her. He'd always been able to cut through the barriers, the distance between her and everyone else.

Only Abby and Sera and Luke had been able to penetrate her defenses.

Bec didn't resent her armor. She'd needed it growing up after losing her mom in childbirth with her baby brother. Left alone with a dad who didn't really want her . . . or maybe that wasn't quite true, but she'd definitely been a poor substitute for his lost wife and son.

They'd moved from the Bay Area to New York for a few years—long enough that Bec no longer sounded purely Californian, long enough that she had a wide streak of New York in her voice. But then her father had moved back to California and . . . he'd left her at school.

Ten years old and stashed in an all-girls boarding school in Upstate New York.

It had been four long years before Sera and Abby had shown up for freshman year and another before Luke had been enrolled in the neighboring all-boys school.

Sera and Abby had basically friended her to death, hadn't left her alone, had pestered and bugged and bothered Bec until she'd relented and become part of a trio instead of a lonely single.

Luke, well, he'd been gorgeous with just a hint of a sexy Southern accent and piercing green eyes her heart hadn't been able to ignore.

No matter the armor and barbed wire.

He'd army-crawled his ass through, wedged himself deep inside.

It had been easier to pretend she'd evicted him from her heart all those years before, but as Sera pointed out, if Bec really *didn't* care about Luke, she never would have agreed to the deal in the first place. He'd only been able to goad her into the agreement because she felt *something*.

And it was time to stop lying to herself.

"How many times did it take you to figure the code out?" she asked as they stepped off of the elevator.

Lips curved. "Three."

She tilted her head. "What were the other dates you tried?"

"Wouldn't you like to know?"

She would. She really would. But obviously, he wanted her to ask, and she couldn't make it *that* easy on him. So, instead of pressing him further, she turned for her door.

"Did you figure out this one, yet?"

He bent, pressed four buttons on the keypad attached to the lock.

It unlatched with a soft *click*.

Oh.

Luke brushed his thumb across her lips. He leaned in, and her chin lifted, wanting his mouth, wanting him to take her into his arms again and kiss her senseless. Hot breath on her forehead, punctuated by a brush of his lips there then the same on her cheek, her jaw, just below her ear before he whispered, "I remember everything about you, sweetheart."

He nudged her over the threshold, quietly closed the door.

"Lock up," he said through the wooden panel.

She did then watched through the peephole as he strode to the elevator. Her phone buzzed just as the metal doors closed.

I can't wait to see you again.

Bec felt the same exact way.

But she was too much of a wuss to reply in kind. Instead, she pulled up her text chain with Sera and asked her friend to meet for apology salads at Molly's the following day.

The reply came in less than a minute.

You're my smartest friend.

A pause.

But just so you know, you owe me apology salads AND apology pastries.

Bec smiled.

Deal.

Her cell buzzed again.

And maybe apology soup.

She snorted.

Done.

"I'm the worst, and you're the best," Bec announced as she sat down in the chair opposite Sera.

Her friend had already been at Molly's for a good amount of time if the paperback, half-eaten salad, and empty glass of water were any indication, and Bec felt another pulse of guilt that she was late to apology salads.

"Well," Sera said, putting a bookmark into her paperback and closing it. "We already know that." She speared another bite of her salad.

"I'm sorry I'm late. I got—"

"Caught up in a case." Sera smiled. "I knew you'd be late. Arriving on time for lunch dates is your arch nemesis. It never fails that you're stopped on the way out of the office."

Since that was exactly what happened, Bec didn't know what to say.

"Pick a soup for us to share. I need an excuse to eat more bread."

Bec glanced at the menu. "Potato and leek?"

"And that's why we're friends." Sera reached across the table and squished Bec's cheeks, tone changing so it sounded like she was talking to a dog. "Because even though you don't like leeks, you'd still order it for me."

Bec smiled. "I don't *hate* them . . ."

"You once called them Satan's pubes of a vegetable."

"That was chives, I'll have you know. And I still stand by *that* statement."

Sera snorted. "Order the tomato, I'll get the leek and we'll live vicariously."

"Good plan." Bec got up to put in the order and then came back to the table with the triangular number placard. And in that amount of time—less than five minutes—realized why Sera had been reading earlier.

Not just because their Sextant loved reading and were ridiculously obsessed with any and all types of romance novels —even Bec wasn't jaded enough to not enjoy a fictional happy ending—but because the book had been a shield against unwanted male attention.

Male attention in the form of the Molly's employee Sera had mentioned the other day.

"Thou art—"

This was Bec's specialty.

She elbowed in between the man-child and Sera then plunked herself on Sera's lap, pressing a smacking kiss to her friend's lips. "There you are, baby."

Sera's shocked expression was worth it.

So. Totally. Worth. It.

In fact, Bec would have documented it for posterity if it wouldn't have blown the cover she was attempting to build.

She unleashed her glare on the man who was more boy than adult. "Leave."

His eyes went wide and his jaw worked for a few seconds before he spun around and left.

Bec pushed out of Sera's lap.

"What. The hell. Was that?" Sera exclaimed as Bec sank down into her own chair.

"You're welcome." Bec waved a judicious hand. "He won't bother you again."

"*Or* he'll get it in his head that he'll want a two-for-one special and then never leave either of us alone again."

Bec turned her head, sent another death glare at the boy who shrank back and hurried through a swinging door into the kitchen. "No, he won't."

Sera smacked her. "Leave poor Timmy alone."

"His name isn't *Timmy*," Bec said. "That's just too . . ."

"Tragic? Charles Dickens? Shakespearean drama?"

"That. Precisely."

A beat before they both cackled.

Sera pointed a finger at her. "I was never an asshole until I met you."

"You're still not an asshole," Bec reminded her. "You're pretty much the nicest person I know. Hence, the necessary rescuing."

Sera opened her mouth, closed it, and sighed before leaning close to Bec and whispering, "Well, I'm sorry to say you're rescuing failed."

Bec frowned when Timmy appeared at her elbow. But he didn't make a pass or even risk eye contact. Instead, he dropped her salad and the two soups onto the table then all but ran away.

She smirked over at Sera. "See? Rescuing *was* successful."

"You're the worst." A shrug, a twitch of Sera's lips. "Or maybe the best. Thanks for making Molly's my safe space again." She fluttered her eyelids, dropped the back of one hand to her forehead. "Oh, Bec Darden, lawyer extraordinaire and possessor of the patented Death Stare, thank you for being my knight in shining armor. Shall I jump aboard your mighty steed and let you carry me away?"

"Sarcasm doesn't suit you." But Bec's lips twitched. "Okay, fine. I'm loving this snarky side of you."

Sera's eyes brightened. "Enough to mount me?" She waggled her brows.

"*Ew.*"

Sera huffed. "Why is it that every single time I make a dirty joke, *that's* the reaction I get from you and the girls? I'm dirty, too! I think about penises and love steamy sex scenes. I can even say"—her voice dropped—"cock."

Bec bursting into laughter. "I'm . . . sorry . . . but you can say *cock*? Oh my God, Sera you are the best."

Sera crossed her arms.

"Careful"—Bec gestured at her boobage area—"or Timmy will forget about my rescuing."

"Bec!"

"Eat, before I get called back to work."

"I need my flipping apology pastry after this abuse," Sera muttered.

Bec reached across the table, squeezed Sera's free hand, and gave her friend what she needed. "Thanks for being my friend."

See? She wasn't *always* an asshole.

Sera's eyes welled up and she dropped her spoon, clasping her hands over her heart. "I *knew* Luke was perfect for you."

Bec scoffed.

Sera stage-whispered, "You have *feelings* now."

"Shut up and eat your apology soup."

"It's *true*," Sera sing-songed.

"Don't tell anyone," Bec grumbled, shoveling her own soup into her mouth. Why had she been nice again? Assholes never had to deal with teasing.

Sera's grin was wide. "It'll be our little secret."

A secret that found its way to the Sextant's group text chain a mere half hour later.

Bec pretended to hate the attention.

But really, she was *secretly* happy that her family cared enough to tease her.

TWELVE

Sera: Bec kissed me!

Abby: *Uh*, what?

Bec: She exaggerates. It was a smack, and I was in pure rescuing mode. Ask her about Timmy.

CeCe: Uh-oh. Timmy from Molly's? What did he do?

Sera: He quoted *Romeo and Juliet*.

Rachel: That sounds romantic, actually.

Bec: She turned him down, and then he began quoting lines from a Shakespearian tragedy. Definitely NOT romantic.

Heather: What does Timmy look like?

Bec: Doesn't matter, he's a drama major.

Abby: *horrified GIF*

Rachel: I second that.

Sera: He wasn't that bad.

Bec: He was worse.

Heather: He sounds worse.

Bec: Hell, yeah he was worse. Plus, he's all of twenty-one.

Sera: Too young for sure and frankly, too weird. But also . . . Luke and Becky sitting in the tree. K-I-S-S-I-N-G.

Bec: I was wrong earlier. YOU'RE the worst.

Sera: *kissing emoji*

Abby: By my count, you've had two dates you haven't dished on.

CeCe: Exactly! I need details.

Rachel: It's my turn to host Wine Night.

Sera: Yes! Wine Night!

Rachel: :) Saturday. I'll kick Sebastian out. Bec bring all the details and the rest of you ALL the books. I need a new read. I'll provide booze and wine.

Bec: You know booze and wine are the same thing.

Rachel: Not to me they aren't.

Abby: I agree. They're two separate food groups.

CeCe: Exactly. Vodka is a veggie and wine a fruit.

Sera: *fist bump gif*

Bec: I'm friends with insane people.

Heather: I can't fault any of CeCe's logic. Stepping into a meeting, so am turning on Do Not Disturb, but I'll be there on Saturday.

CeCe: Me too. Colin and I are back from Scotland on Friday!

Abby: I'm boring and have no social life, aside from you ladies. Of course, I'll see you then.

Rachel: What she said. ^^

Sera: Ditto ^

Bec: Fine. Saturday.

Sera: Unless she has a date with Luuuuuke.

Abby: *rolling on the floor laughing GIF*

Rachel: Haha. Nice.

CeCe: *slow clap GIF*

Heather: Get back to work, ladies. *fist bump emoji* That's for you, Sera.

Bec: I hate you all.

THIRTEEN

Luke

HE'D KNOWN this was bound to happen.

"I'm sorry," Becky said, and though her tone was laced with an apology, it also held a hard edge.

She was expecting him to be mad.

Like he used to be.

"Switch to FaceTime," he told her.

"What?"

Luke pulled the phone from his ear, pressed the button so he could see his Becky's face.

After a few seconds, it appeared on the screen.

Her blonde hair swept up into a messy ponytail, a pale blue silky tank top giving him a tantalizing view of her braless state. Fuck, she was beautiful.

"Sweetheart," he said. "Look at me."

Lips pressing together, she put what looked to be a toiletry bag down. "What?"

Ice in her voice now. Definitely expecting a fight. Or a guilt trip. He'd been good at those, too.

"It's okay."

She huffed. "I *know* it's okay. My job is important, and sometimes—"

"Sometimes it takes priority." Luke wished they were having this conversation in person rather than over the phone so he could tug her close and make her understand that this time everything between them was different. "Sweetheart, *stop*."

Gray eyes met his.

"We'll reschedule."

Hope danced across her face. "Yeah?"

"Of course, we will," he told her. "I need to fly back to Texas to take care of a few things actually."

"Oh, I didn't realize." White teeth nibbled at her bottom lip. "Is everything okay?"

He shrugged. "Yeah. I've been wanting to break into renewables in California. We've been looking for prospective sites in the Central Valley to try out some new technology our engineers have developed. I need to go back to the board with my proposals."

Becky picked up the toiletry bag again, and Luke spent a few moments staring at the ceiling while she stashed it in her suitcase. "You should talk to Heather."

"Who's Heather?"

She blew a strand of hair off her forehead, walking with the phone into the closet and pulling out a red power suit. "Heather O'Keith—"

"From RoboTech?" he asked, shocked. "We've been trying to set up a meeting with her for ages."

"Well, I think I can help you with that," Becky said. "For a price."

Luke grinned. "What price?"

"I get to plan our next date."

That grin faded.

"Becky—"

"Bec," she corrected. "And no negotiations either. You've had entirely too much control over this dating situation already."

"I don't see anything wrong with that."

Zip, went the garment bag. Up, went one of her eyebrows.

"We've had fun, haven't we?" he asked.

"I did like scoring more than you in ax throwing."

"Allegedly," he corrected.

The other brow went up. "Clearly, I won by ten points."

"You stepped over the line!" she said, lifting her suitcase to the floor and draping the garment bag on top of it before flopping onto her bed.

"Did not."

"The last throw didn't count."

"Did so."

"*Ugh.*"

"Sugar pie?"

"What?" she snapped, and Luke felt a blip of happiness when she didn't correct his use of the nickname.

"I like arguing with you."

She froze, lips curving up. "You're annoying."

"Of course, I am."

A shake of her head. "What am I going to do with you?"

"Keep me?"

Becky sighed even though her eyes danced. "Let me plan the next date, and I'll consider it."

"Relentless." A beat. "I wish you'd let me drive you to the airport."

"I have a driver," she said. "And my flight leaves at five. It's awful."

"He won't give you the goodbye kiss I will."

She tapped a finger to her chin. "Maybe. Maybe not."

"You fight dirty."

A shrug.

"Fine. You get to plan Date Three, but only if you let me come over in the morning and drive you to the airport," he added as her expression turned victorious. "I need to prove to you that I can kiss better than your driver."

Becky shook her head. "And you say *I'm* relentless." But her mouth was curved into a smile. "Fine. But be forewarned, I need to leave at three-thirty."

"I'll be there." She stifled a yawn and Luke smiled. "I'll let you get some sleep."

She snuggled into the blankets of her bed. "'Kay."

"Becky?"

"Hmm?"

Another blip of happiness as she let his *Becky* slip by.

"I like negotiating with you."

"I like *negotiating* with you too, Pearson," she said, eyes sliding closed.

Even though he'd just talked himself into getting less than four hours of sleep, when Luke hung up, he had the biggest smile on his face.

LUKE LIPS BURNED as he watched his Becky stride away, her hips swaying, rolling the small black suitcase behind her as she strode toward the private jet that was waiting on the tarmac. A flight attendant carried her garment bag, had tried to take the suitcase as well, but Becky had waved him off. Luke had watched the other man bend close and then laugh loudly at something *his* Becky had said.

Fucking bastard.

Luke wanted to be the man Becky talked to. The *only* man.

And that thought was staying exactly where it should, locked deep within his possessive caveman brain.

She walked up the steps, pausing just at the door. His heart leaped when she turned toward his car and waved. Luke waved back, though realistically he knew it was too dark outside for her to see through the windows.

Then she was gone, and he needed to drive back to his empty hotel room.

He missed her more in that moment than in their decade apart. Before he'd been used to not being with his Becky, had used anger to cauterize those wounds inside him. This—hope for a second chance, wishing their relationship worked out, wanting a future with her—was different.

Those old wounds ached.

His phone buzzed.

Get a move on, Pearson. I'll see you in a week.

Luke's mouth curved.

That date better be impressive.

The plane's door slammed closed, the stairs rolled away.

You doubt me?

His fingers flew across his screen.

Bec Fucking Darden? Hell, no. I'd bet on you anytime, sweetheart. Safe flight.

She sent back a GIF of a giggling movie star, and he was

smiling as he watched her plane take off, knowing his heart might as well be in the seat next to her.

This time around, Luke would wait for her, however long it took.

MONDAY of the next week rolled around bright and early, and Luke was beyond relieved to be meeting with Heather O'Keith.

If only because it meant he was getting out of his hotel room.

The maid had given him such a pitying look yesterday afternoon, after he'd refused a cleaning for the third day in a row. So what if he'd answered the door in a ratty T-shirt and boxer briefs, his hair a mess? He'd put all the dirty room service dishes outside in the hall. He'd taken the proffered clean towels.

Maybe he hadn't *used* them . . .

Okay, so he was a disgusting mess.

But not *this* morning because he'd caught up with all the outstanding Pearson Energy business, had put the finishing touches on his plan for what he was considering doing in California with his renewable trials, and he'd put on a suit.

Oh. He'd also showered.

And left his room for coffee that didn't come with a twenty percent markup.

Take that, judgy cleaning lady.

He'd even grabbed a coffee for Heather—pinging Becky for her favorite, so never let it be said that he wasn't going full-board with wanting to make a good impression on the CEO of Robo-Tech. He didn't typically chase connections, happy with his medium slice of the pie, but this was *Heather O'Keith.* She was a hugely successful businesswoman—her multi-billion-dollar corporation could eat Pearson Energy for breakfast—and fucking up with her wouldn't bode well for the future of his company.

But that wasn't the only reason. Luke was also putting in extra effort because she was Becky's close friend.

He didn't want to disappoint either of them.

It would also be nice if Heather liked him, at least a little bit.

He checked in at the security desk, received a temporary badge, and was told to have a seat in the lobby area. Rachel, Heather's assistant, would be down in a few minutes to collect him.

Luke's ass had barely touched the leather before a woman with warm brown hair and eyes and a lovely smile stepped off the elevator and strode toward him. He stood when it became clear he was her target and shook her hand.

"You must be Rachel."

She nodded, eyes tracing over him in a way that was completely assessing and yet also completely absent of sexual interest. "I am." A beat. "So, Luke Pearson, you're the one who got our calm, cool, and self-assured Bec so riled up."

"*My* Becky is perfectly capable of kicking anyone who riles her up straight to the curb."

One finger tapped her chin. "Hmm. Then why is she keeping *you* around?"

Luke grinned. "No clue. But I'm going to do my best to *stay* around."

"You'll do, Pearson. I just think you'll do." Rachel inclined her head in the direction of the elevators. "Come on. Heather's just finishing up with a call."

Thirty minutes later, he was packing up his briefcase with a huge smile on his face. The woman hadn't disappointed. She was brilliant and a straight-shooter, even pointing out several flaws in his project that he'd missed and would need to be addressed before the project rolled out, but RoboTech would be happy to be an investor in the venture.

Luke was glad he'd postponed his flight back to Texas until that evening. Her green light meant he could get the board to vote on the project while he was there, and then he and his team would be able to get started.

His initial thoughts had been rolling out the trials in six to eight months, but RoboTech's involvement and the infrastructure they already had in place—including several warehouses and a laboratory in the Central Valley—meant that his timeline would be less than half that.

For the first time in years, Luke wasn't in survival mode, wasn't doing something because he was obligated or trying to save his family. He was excited about work.

Heather stopped him with a hand on his shoulder. "Luke."

He glanced up at her. "Sorry, my mind was racing ahead with ideas. Did you have anything else you wanted to discuss?"

"Yes."

His gut sank. *Shit.* Maybe she was having second thoughts.

"Is it the storage numbers? My engineers truly think they can transfer it to the batteries at a rate of ninety-five percent."

Heather waved a hand. "I'll have my team confirm all the calculations before rollout. I'm sure they're competent, but . . . never mind. This isn't so much business as it's Bec." Eyes narrowing, she fixed him in place with a glare.

His gut sank further.

"You hurt my friend." She crossed her arms.

"I—" He sighed. "I was a fucking ass. I let the best thing in my world slip through my fingers."

"Hmm." Those arms stayed crossed, those eyes still narrowed.

He did some narrowing of his own. "Becky has decided to give me a second chance to prove I've grown out of my asshole tendencies, and I'm not giving it up." She opened her mouth, but he pressed on. "And if that's why you're investing in this project—to get me to walk away from the best thing in my life—well, fuck it because business doesn't mean as much to me as my Becky does."

"Hmm," she said again.

His temper spiked. Was this just a waste of his time? A way to test him and find him lacking?

"You know what?" He thrust the file with the tentative contract offer at her. "Fuck this. I love Becky. Always have, always will. I'm not leaving her." Furious, he started for the elevators.

"Luke." She caught his arm again.

"I'm not using her—"

"I don't believe I accused you of that."

Her calm tone finally penetrated his temper, and he thought back at her words. Heather *hadn't* given any indication of thinking he was using Becky for her connections. Nope. That was all him.

He winced. "I'm fucking this up, aren't I?"

A flash of white as Heather grinned. "Not as badly as you think. I like that you're defensive of Bec—or *Becky* as you call her. She deserves someone who cares enough to fight for her." She squeezed his arm. "Your Becky isn't a weakling. She'll chew up and spit out anyone spineless."

Luke raised a brow. "I'm not going to let her push me away."

"See that you don't." Heather handed him the file back. "I almost lost the best thing that ever happened to me because I was too scared to jump. Take my advice, and just dive in."

He snorted. "Good advice if I wasn't already in over my head. Fuck, if I don't love her to the moon and back—" He shook his head. "Damn, what kind of drugs did you put in the water you served me? Because I did *not* just say that."

"No drugs," Rachel teased, joining them. "Just the power of the *hmm*." Her voice dropped to a stage whisper. "It's her tactic. Gets even the most recalcitrant of peeps to dish all."

"Don't give all my secrets away." Heather smacked her. "You're supposed to be on *my* side, remember?"

Rachel smirked, leading the way toward the elevators. "This one is going to need all the help he can get if he's going to take down our *Becky*."

Oh, he was going to be in so much trouble with this Becky thing.

"True," Heather said with a nod.

They said their goodbyes, and he got onto the elevator when it stopped on their floor.

"Oh, Luke?" Heather asked.

He paused, finger on the button, holding the doors open.

"Next time you talk to Bec, ask her about the time she kissed Sera."

His brows drew together, his finger slipped off the white circle. "Did you say kis—?"

The panels slid closed to the sound of Rachel and Heather's cackling.

Well, he couldn't let that information stand without immediate action. He texted Becky and laughed out loud when her response came before he'd reached the lobby.

I'm suing the lot of them for defamation.

He strode out of the elevator, headed for his rental car.

Is this the point I shouldn't mention you've now made one of my top fantasies come true?

And instead of the sass he'd been expecting, Luke got heat.

What are the other fantasies?

He took a breath, glared down at his cock, mentally threatening it to behave.

Come home and I'll show you.

The selfie she sent in reply had his cock hardening further, regardless of his previous threat. Her hair was down, eyes sultry, lips red and lush, and her tank top positioned low enough that her nipples were almost exposed.

I thought of you just this morning.

Had she–? Did she mean—?
Luke's brain wouldn't even work in complete sentences.

Two more days.

Thank fuck for that.

FOURTEEN

Bec

SHE WAS UNACCOUNTABLY NERVOUS.

Like stupidly nervous.

Harvard law graduate, and she was afraid of a pizza date.

But Luke was going to be there in five minutes, and . . . she was wearing short-shorts. Why had she thought it was a good idea to squeeze into them again? She wasn't twenty-one, and they weren't on the beach eating cold pizza and drinking warm beer. Things had shifted. Her legs weren't as lean, her waist not as trim.

Hell, if she sat down, she'd have rolls.

"That's life, Darden," she muttered. "Plus, real women have rolls. It's a fact of—"

"What's this about rolls?"

A masculine voice that sent a shiver down her spine.

She turned, saw Luke standing just inside her door. He was wearing those faded jeans and a tight green T-shirt that brought out the emerald streaks in his eyes. Eyes that heated as he looked her over, down and then back up. His gaze was hot, scorching her as it took in every inch of her exposed skin.

And considering she was wearing a very skimpy bikini top to go with the short-shorts, it was a *lot* of exposed skin.

"Turn around," he said, hoarsely.

"What?"

He swallowed hard. "Please, baby. If you care about me even the tiniest amount, please, *please* turn around."

Frowning, Bec rotated so her back was to him.

"Oh, thank you Jesus." She glanced over her shoulder, saw his stare go from hot to scorching. "I think you dropped something."

Bec had bent to glance down at the ground before she realized that he was messing with her. "Pig," she accused, straightening with a glare despite her lips twitching and betraying her amusement.

"Those shorts should receive a fucking Oscar."

She laughed.

Ten seconds in Luke's presence and she'd forgotten all about rolls.

She knew feeling this way—sexier, less self-conscious because of a few words and a hot look—meant she should probably turn in her feminist card. She *knew* that other people's opinions shouldn't matter and that a man appreciating her body shouldn't have any bearing on how she felt about herself, but dammit, sometimes having someone look at her and *not* see all the flaws her inner critic loved to point out felt really fucking good.

Luke wasn't worried about her legs or hips or stomach.

Luke thought she was beautiful.

And somehow, that made it easier for her to see herself that way, too.

Bec knew she projected confidence to the world, that no one

would suspect she was self-conscious or insecure, but . . . some-times that protective armor got really heavy to carry.

Sometimes she wanted someone to appreciate the person she was . . . on the inside *and* outside.

Rolls or not.

Warm hands slid around her waist, his slightly roughened palms making her shiver. "Why aren't you wearing any clothes?"

She rested her head on his chest, cuddling close, loving the feel of his fingers skating up and down her spine. "My twenty-first birthday." His arms tightened, his body—lies, his *cock*—hardened, pressing against her stomach. "I didn't bring in any sand, but I do have the pizza and beer."

"I think I'm still finding sand in places I shouldn't," he teased.

"Hence, apartment picnicking on the 'beach'"—she made air quotes then pointed to her TV, which was displaying a screen-saver of the ocean—"rather than the real beach."

"Thank you," he murmured.

She shrugged. "It's not much, but I—"

"It's *everything*. Thank you." He cupped her jaw in his palm. "I missed you."

And Bec knew he hadn't just missed her body or the skimpy clothes or even the sass she constantly threw his way.

He'd missed *her*.

Talking to her, being with her . . . *all* of her.

Click.

That locked box hiding in the depths of her heart was open—dangerously, wonderfully open.

She rose up on tiptoe and kissed him.

There was no hesitation in Luke's response. He tightened his hold and slipped his tongue between her lips, teasing her with a rhythm she remembered instinctually. They'd honed it over the years, perfected the caresses, the timing, the pressure, the speed.

And just like it had a decade before, that rhythm took her from mildly turned on to almost insane with need. One leg hitched around his waist, and she all but climbed into his arms, desperate to get closer, rubbing herself against him, groaning into his mouth.

"Baby," he said, gently clasping the tops of her arms and setting her away from him. "We should slow down."

The thing about her itty-bitty bikini top was that it was flimsy. One tug of the right string and it would end up on the floor. Bec never wore it in public for just that reason. In fact, the only time she'd ever worn it—not including this time in her living room—was with Luke.

Paired with these same shorts.

When she was skinnier (a.k.a. had yet to grow boobs).

Today? A good fifteen pounds heavier—hence, *rolls*—and she was threatening to pop right out of it.

Her intent was exactly that, of course. She'd given Luke too much power in their relationship, too much control in deciding when to come back, when to go on dates, how far they were going to go.

Bec was in this now.

She'd made peace with going for Luke and all the potential heartache that might follow in his wake.

And so, dammit, that meant she was taking some control back.

Also, she really needed an orgasm that didn't come as a result of her own handiwork, *pun intended.*

"Pearson," she said and arched her back deliberately, slipping one hand up her back and tugging. His eyes went huge as the bikini top slid to the floor. "Just in case you were wondering,

I was hoping we'd celebrate with cold pizza and warm beer later."

He was frozen, jaw in a tight line, his hands still on her arms. "Becky—"

"Bec," she corrected, grabbing his wrists and placing his hands over her breasts. They both groaned at the sensation, his fingers flexing and causing little zings of pleasure to extend right down in between her thighs. "And by later, I meant *much* later, after you give me multiple orgasms and remind me how good your cock"—she reached down and squeezed the hard length of him—"feels inside of me."

"I—"

She placed one finger over his lips. "Now's the time to shut up and kiss me."

He nipped that fingertip, making her jump as more sparks of pleasure coursed down between her legs. She was wet and aching and—

Luke swept her up into his arms, carrying her over to the blanket, but when he would have set her on the square of checkered material, Bec tugged at his shoulders. "Wait."

A painful expression crossed his face. "Second thoughts," he said and gave a tight nod. "We'll wait—"

This man.

She never felt like this with anyone else—never was tender and protective, never felt her heart actually pinch with the urge to make things better for him.

She'd never *loved* another man.

Never.

The thought made her panic for a moment, to consider actually stopping, but then she remembered this was Luke, and Luke was different.

And *she* was different with Luke.

So, Bec put her lawyer mind to work. She tucked away those

feelings—the panic, the relief, the hope, and the anticipation—and promised herself she'd spend plenty of time analyzing them later. That complete, she tugged Luke's head down until his mouth met hers.

Only when her lungs burned and her heart was threatening to pound itself right out of her chest did she break away.

"I was just going to say, how about going to the bedroom?" Her head rested against his shoulder, and he still cradled her against his chest. "I'm too old to have sex on barely padded hardwood floor."

Luke's body went stiff, but before Bec had a chance to worry she'd said the wrong thing—and face it, she often *did* say the wrong thing—she realized he was laughing.

"Fuck, but I love you," he said in between breaths. "I can never, *ever* predict what is going to come out of your mouth."

That panic from before?

When she'd realized how much she still cared for—loved, okay, okay *loved*—Luke, well that panic she'd tucked away to deal with later reared its ugly head. He loved her? She loved him? How long would it last? When would she do or say something to make things change, to make Luke angry again?

Or maybe she'd run away again. Be pathetic and cowardly and—

No.

No more.

If she'd learned anything over the last decade, it was how to be fearless. She hadn't had therapy, not like Luke, hadn't been open to such a course in the past, not when every time she made herself vulnerable, things around her went to shit.

Her work had been her therapy. The one thing to not let her down. She could be terrified, but if she was always prepared, if she devoted herself and practically lived in the office, feeding off the cases, if she just worked her ass off, then she could be successful, dammit.

And it had worked.

Eventually she'd been able to weave those slender tendrils of confidence into something larger. She'd found faith in herself, knew she was smart and capable, knew she could be fucking brilliant.

And now, this was her chance.

She'd managed to be fearless in her professional life, managed to carve out happiness there, with her friends and as thus, she could damn well carry that fearlessness over into her personal life.

So, instead of pushing Luke away, Bec shoved the terror of the situation down and tugged him closer. Instead of throwing those words back at him in angry, hurtful bites, she tucked them into that empty space in her heart.

One day, she vowed, one day she might even believe them.

One day . . . she might find herself worthy of them.

One day—

Enough.

Today was here and now, and if Bec had learned nothing else through this whole painful endeavor, it was that she had to live for today.

"I love you," she said. "I don't think I've ever stopped loving you. I hated you. I loathed you. I wanted to put your balls in a meat grinder"—she grinned at his expression—"but I think I always loved you, Luke Pearson. Even when I didn't want to."

Then before he could reply, before she lost her nerve, Bec kissed him again.

"Make love to me," she murmured against his lips. "Please."

Emerald eyes met hers, warm but searching for long moments. Luke swallowed hard, eyes darting away from Bec long enough that her heart started to sink. At least until she heard his words. "Which one of those many white doors leads to your bedroom?"

Bec grinned, because she knew the hall *did* have a lot of doors. Four in one corner of her apartment, in fact—one leading to her bedroom, another to a half bathroom, there was also a linen closet and her washer-dryer.

She debated for a heartbeat, thinking of several ways to tease him.

Game show model presenting doors.

Her version of whack-a-mole, only with guess-the-door instead.

Hot-cold-hotter-colder.

Then the arm holding the upper half of her body shifted, sliding around her rib cage, calloused fingers brushing along her side, grazing the underside of one breast, rubbing over the top of her nipple.

Stars flashed behind her eyes.

Luke bent, sucked that nipple into his mouth, and made her forget about her plans to tease him. "Which door?" he asked again, releasing her and straightening.

"I—"

Another brush of that thumb and really, if driving her insane with need was a sport then Luke Pearson definitely excelled at it.

"Door, sugar pie," he said again, walking toward the hall.

"Second on the left."

He shifted her body so he could turn the knob and opened the correct door. A bare heartbeat later, she was flat on her back with him on top of her.

One long, slow drag of his tongue up her abdomen, up her sternum, and then over, back to her breast, back to the aching points of her nipples. "You're so fucking beautiful," he told her.

"It's the short-shorts," she managed to joke, even though his tongue was teasing her breasts and she was slowly going insane.

Never let it be said that Bec Darden lost her cool. She was calm and composed—

Except when Luke did that thing with his tongue.

Because any hope of composure went straight out the window.

Luckily, Luke didn't seem to mind in the least.

FIFTEEN

Luke

HE'D BEEN SHOWN UP. He knew it. Fuck, the whole universe knew he'd been bested by a checkered blanket and a bright red bikini top.

But Luke found it didn't bother him at all.

Not when she was half-naked beneath him, skin like silken fire. He wanted to touch her all over, to stroke and kiss and lick every inch of her, but he also needed to be sure she wasn't rushing this, that she was as fully into this as he was—

Luke snorted.

Becky froze, glanced up at him. "What?"

"I was going around in my head why this both is *and isn't* a good idea." Her eyes started to dim, and he grabbed her hand, dragging it down his cock, which was threatening to break in half. "I want you. Don't *ever* doubt that, okay?" He waited until she nodded. "I was worried you were doing something you didn't want."

She raised a brow.

"Hence, the snort." He nuzzled at her neck. "My Becky doesn't do anything she doesn't want, least of all me."

"Your *Bec*," she said. "And sidenote, I'm going to get you back for all this *Becky* talk. My friends have sent me no less than a million Valley girl GIFS. I think I need to resurrect the Lucky Luke nickname."

He shuddered. "Please God, no."

She shoved at his shoulders. "Then you'd better strip me out of these short ass shorts and spend some quality time between my thighs."

"Oh, really?" Luke let his fingers drift down her abdomen, dip under the waistband of those shorts. Becky shivered, hips shifting restlessly. "You want my mouth?"

Feminine hands darted between them, undid the button, slid down the zipper. "I seem to remember you could do some really impressive things with your mouth, Pearson."

"Hmm."

A kiss just above her belly button then below.

"Now you sound like Heather."

"Shh." A nip to her hip bone. "I don't want to think about Heather. I want to think about how good your pussy is going to taste." He punctuated his statement by tugging off her shorts and underwear then dragging one finger between her wet folds.

Her breath caught when he brought it up to his mouth and sucked, closing his eyes as the sweet tang hit his tongue. She spread her thighs further, tilted her hips.

"*Luke.*"

An invitation.

One that he didn't need an engraved postcard to heed.

He tossed her legs over his shoulders, and she wove her hands into his hair, yanked his mouth against her pussy, and ground herself against him.

Suddenly, Luke wasn't thinking about teasing any longer.

Or at least not *him* being teased. His woman on the other hand . . .

He figured he had about ten years' worth of time to make up for.

Thus, he pulled out every trick he possessed, everything he knew Becky had liked in the past, every technique he'd learned and perfected since then. He licked and kissed and nipped, concentrating all his efforts on making her feel good, on driving her to the edge of reason, on propelling her straight to an orgasm.

Fingers in his hair, the grip bordering on painful, but Luke didn't give a damn, not when he had his Becky wet and hot against his mouth.

"Oh, my God—"

Thighs clamped around his head, her spine arched off the mattress, and she screamed his name.

He brought her down, slowing the movements of his tongue and fingers, helping her descend the peak, continuing to kiss her as her movements calmed . . . and not stopping until she was writhing against him again, gripping his hair, cursing him out.

And then he just used his fingers.

He kept them on her clit, circling, pressing, slipping down and inside, because his mouth was otherwise occupied.

As in he needed to get it on her breasts.

Her nipples were hard little points, and he sucked one into his mouth. "Luke— *Oh God!* Mmm, baby. I—" He switched sides, slid another finger into the heat of her, curling them up and forward, rubbing against her G-spot, feeling moisture pool around him.

"Oh *fuck*," she gasped. "Oh fuck, oh fuck, oh—"

She clamped down hard around his fingers, and Luke almost went over the edge with her. It had been *so fucking long*, and watching her come—seeing the pink spreading across her cheeks, the tops of her breasts, a sheen of sweat glistening on her forehead—was absolutely beautiful.

She was beautiful.

Especially, when her eyes opened and focused on him with lazy awareness. Swollen lips tipped upward into a smile. "You'll do, Pearson. You'll do."

He twitched his fingers—the ones still deep inside her. "You sure?" Another twitch that made her gasp and her pussy pulse around him. "Because I think"—he started moving, slow and gentle and in a rhythm that would soon have her climbing that peak again—"I might still need to prove myself to you."

His thumb drifted up—

"Touch my clit and die."

Luke laughed. He was fully dressed with a naked Becky and had a boner that could easily substitute for a hammer, and he was laughing.

Using his free hand, he cupped her cheek. "How did I ever let you go?"

Regret, and this time no pun was intended, *hammered* into him. But dammit, he'd wasted so much fucking time.

"Hey."

One sharp word of a sound, surprising his eyes into meeting hers.

"I think we've been over this already." Beck gripped his wrist, slid his fingers from her, lips parting in a silent protest before she shook her head and seemed to regain herself. "The past is the past, and we're going to move forward. Going to try and—"

"See," he said, moving up on the bed and lying down next to her. "It's not that simple—"

"Ugh." She threw her hands up. "You're ruining my orgasm afterglow."

"Uh—"

"We fucked up, okay?" she said, pushing up and jabbing him in the chest with one red-painted fingernail. "*Both* of us. That's the way this works."

"I was—"

"Oh, so are we going to play Who Was the Bigger Asshole now?" she snapped. "Really? Because I'm pretty sure we both would win that top prize." When he opened his mouth, she hurried to say, "Did you tell me to go? Yes. Did I say a lot of shitty stuff before that? *Fuck yes*."

Luke blinked.

"Forgot about that part?" She huffed. "Yeah. Thought so. Luke, you were jealous of my success in part because I rubbed it in. I was hurt you weren't as happy for me about the job as you should have been, so I talked about it every chance I got. I made you feel inadequate and—"

He caught her hand. "That's bullshit, and you know it. If I'd been supportive like a real husband should have been—"

"And there's another *should have*." She tugged her hand free, popped up from the mattress, and started pacing the room in all her naked glory. Or, it *would* have been glorious, if her words didn't slice to the center of him. "How convenient. You get to play the martyr and shoulder the blame for everything, and then we never work out what was truly wrong with our relationship."

His heart skipped a beat.

Because, dammit, his therapist had said much of the same thing. Absorbing blame was one way to take control of a situation, but it was also a way to push people away. To sacrifice himself for their good.

Even if such a sacrifice wasn't for the betterment of the people involved.

He cleared his throat, shoved down the urge to keep arguing

that everything was *his* fault and forced himself to ask, "What was wrong with us?"

"Communication, Luke." She stopped, stared at him. "Even now, we both have all of these feelings that are tearing us up inside and we're masking them with apologies and sex and cute date nights that only relive the good stuff." Becky crossed back over to him and sat on the edge of the mattress. "We're forgetting the hard days. The disagreements and blaring arguments, and . . . we're forgetting what made us *us*."

He slipped off his shirt then tugged it over her head. "That tore us apart. Before."

A nod. "It did."

"I'm not going to let it drag us back down," he said. "But I also can't just pretend that I didn't fuck up."

She touched his jean-clad leg. "The important point is that we *both* fucked up. That's the part you need to accept."

Luke froze. "It goes against everything in me to let someone else take the blame."

A smile. "I know."

"But it's also the truth. We both made mistakes and if we want to move forward . . ."

"We have to let that go."

He swallowed hard. "I don't want to hurt you again."

Becky curled into his side. "I understand now." A smile. "*Finally*, I get it. We can't go back and fix everything from before, but we *can* build something strong now. It's only . . ."

"I don't like the sound of that."

"I worry if we can't stop focusing on how things were and all the mistakes we made, I worry we'll be destined to—" She broke off, shook her head.

"I'm keeping you," he said. "So tough shit with the psychological stuff or the destined to fall apart nonsense. The one thing I learned in therapy was that I have never stopped loving you—"

"Then just be the Luke I know you can be," she said. "If you love me, then stop hurting yourself. Because, *fuck*, it hurts me so much when you do that."

He dropped his chin to his chest, sighed. "I hate it when you're smarter than me."

She laughed, that lovely laugh that filled him up with helium from the inside out. "Face facts, Pearson. You love me because I am smarter than you."

"Not hard to do."

Becky dropped her head to his shoulder. "I admit that I was recalcitrant at first, scared of getting hurt again, but that in and of itself was the truth of it. No other man I've met is capable of getting close enough to wound me."

His heart skipped a beat. "That's a dubious honor if I've ever heard one."

"Don't you see?" she said, pushing up with one on his chest so she could stare down at him. "Don't you know you're the only man to ever penetrate the armor around my heart? Don't you understand that you're the only one who ever mattered?"

Luke's throat was tight, and his eyes burned suspiciously. "Come here."

He tugged Becky close, turning them so they were lying long ways on the bed and then he held her, turning over the words in his mind, replaying their years together, studying their mistakes. He did so not as a way to flagellate himself with the multitude of regrets and *should haves*. Instead, he remembered the good times and the bad. Together. As pieces of an entire puzzle that formed a picture in color rather than black and white, rather than past equaled bad.

Instead, he saw *everything*.

Imperfect as it was.

And for the first time in his life, he wasn't worrying about measuring up to some perfect image his father or family wanted him to be. He wasn't worrying about being the perfect boyfriend or spouse.

Finally, Luke was free to be himself.

He shucked his jeans, tugged the covers up and over them, a huge weight lifted from his chest. Becky snuggled right against his side, her hair tickling his nose, floral scent surrounding him like the softest blanket.

She was wearing his shirt and as a result of just holding her, he was sporting a boner the size of Georgia and . . . he didn't care.

Because Becky was in his arms at last.

He kissed the top of her head, eyes beginning to close, her breathing slowing, evening out—

"I'm the only man to *penetrate* you?"

Without missing a beat, without even lifting her head, she pinched him just above the nipple. "Pig."

"*Ouch!*"

"Sorry," she said, her tone conveying the opposite. The fingers that had pinched him, drifted down his chest lazily. "I should—"

He caught that wandering hand, pressed a kiss to the palm.

"You should sleep and let me hold you."

She sighed. "Fine."

But Luke felt her smile against his shoulder.

"Your therapist sucked."

He laughed. "You should have seen me before."

"I *did* see you before."

"Really?" He ran his fingers through her hair. "And you say *I'm* the worst?"

"We can share the mantle." She snuggled close, traced circles on his chest.

"I'd share anything with you, sugar pie."

"Lucky Luke," she warned.

"Did you ever—" He stopped.

One eyelid peeled back. "Did I what?"

"Did you talk to someone too?" he asked. "I mean, we both have textbook daddy issues, but you're significantly better adjusted than I am."

Her mouth curved. "That's because I'm awesome. It's also not true." The smile faded. "I'm still—not screwed up exactly, and I am in a better place. But I have this hole in my heart and I'm not sure it will ever go away."

"Sweetheart." His own heart hurt for her.

"I just always wanted things to be different between my dad and me—" She blinked, her tone becoming more businesslike, less sad. "But actually, hearing that you went to therapy kind of makes me want to try it myself." She pressed her palm to his chest. "Not right now, but eventually, maybe it might be good to talk with someone."

"I think that sounds very mature."

She made a face. "Gross." But then she laughed, and he found himself chuckling along with her. "I wasn't in the right head space to talk to anyone before now. I was just lucky to have Abby and Sera and now the rest of the girls and honestly, the rest of it came from work. Work got me through a lot of the darkness. Helping other people, feeling like I had some worth in this world because I could get them some recompense. And, eventually, I was able to believe that was true."

"You're amazing."

She snuggled against him again. "Lies."

"Not lies. The truth."

A sigh, but a relaxed one rather than annoyance for a change. "If you insist."

"I do insist," he said and wrapped his arms around, letting his eyes slide closed, enjoying the feel of her next to him, the scent of wildflowers and sunshine teasing his nose. "Sweetheart?" he asked a few minutes later.

"Mmm?"

"Thank you."

"Anytime, Pearson. Anytime."

They tumbled headfirst into sleep, waking up hours later to eat cold pizza and drink warm beer as they binged on bad reality TV. It was different from ten years ago, but Luke decided that was perfectly—*imperfectly*—fine with him.

SIXTEEN

Becky—er Bec

INTERNAL REVELATIONS WERE EXHAUSTING.

Bec prided herself on not filtering, on being the type of person who existed without artifice. There was a reason she didn't date, why her father could barely stand the sight of her. But she'd been kidding herself when it came to Luke.

As in she'd tried to pretend that she was going to casually give their relationship another go, like one might try on a different shade of red lipstick.

But she should have known that things would get complicated.

Hell, just picking the right shade of red lipstick was really fucking hard.

Categorizing Luke was harder.

Or *had* been harder.

Because after last night . . . things had changed.

She glanced up at him sleeping. They'd tumbled back into her bed with pleasantly full stomachs, eyes burning from too much B-list celebrity drama, and had promptly passed out.

But now it was after seven. She was wide awake and needed to go in to work.

And . . . she didn't want to move from Luke's arms.

They'd each revealed something last night, and she didn't know how she'd survived the discomfort of it.

Then why did you demand complete honesty and communication?

Because, clearly, I'm a fucking idiot.

Yup. Arguments with herself at seven in the morning, she was so fucking together.

"I can smell the smoke from here."

Bec blinked, glanced up, and found Luke's gorgeous green eyes on her. "What?" she blurted and . . . *so fucking smooth.* But it was hard to be her usual calm and put together self when she felt like she should be running, pulling all those pieces of armor back around her, stitching them tightly together. It had been so easy last night to lay it all out there, but in the light of the morning?

Not so much.

Luke shifted, sliding down on the bed so their faces were level. "Good morning."

And he kissed her, ignoring all signs of morning breath—and hers was no doubt horrible, after their three A.M. booty call with pizza and beer—slipping his tongue past the threshold of her lips and giving her a thoroughly dizzying wakeup call.

Eventually, he broke away, both of them breathing hard.

"I knew you'd be doing this."

Her brows drew down. "Doing what?"

"Freaking."

She started to protest, but there was something in his expression—as though he were expecting her to withdraw—and that smug expectation gave her the courage to push on.

The bastard probably knew it, too.

Ugh.

"Fine. I *am* freaking out," she said. "But only a little bit." He snorted. "I'm not used to this. To feeling like *this*—"

Smugness faded from his face. "It would probably be better if I left you alone, let you get back to your own life—"

Just the words made Bec's heart throb. She wouldn't let him leave her, not now, not when things were different—and not even just with the two of them, but also within her.

She felt different. Inside.

Fuck all this noble shit. She wanted Luke, and even though it scared her so damned much, she was keeping him.

Sorry, not sorry. That was just the way it was—

"But I can't," he said.

She blinked, the argument she'd been whipping up inside her brain promptly fading away. "Good," she said. "Because I'm not letting you go."

His eyes warmed. "Possessive little thing, aren't you?"

"You're only a few inches taller than me, Pearson. I wouldn't push your luck."

Fingers traced down her neck, her arm, sliding to a stop on the bare skin of her hip. "I'm six inches taller, at least."

She raised a brow, doing some sliding of her own. "Sorry to say, but *six* inches isn't going to cut it." She followed the trail of hair that began at his belly button and disappeared beneath the waistband of his boxer briefs.

"It's not the"—he broke off with a hiss as she ran a fingertip over his cock—"size that counts."

Her mouth curved. "But how you use it?"

"Exact—*fuck*." She stroked him from base to tip.

"Mmm." Bec pushed up on her elbow, watching his face as she glided her hand up and down. His eyes were squeezed tight, his jaw clamped, his hips jerked off the mattress, pressing closer to her hand. Moisture pooled between her thighs as she stroked him up and down, up and down, up and—

Strong fingers on her wrist, staying her movements.

"Luke—"

The rest of her sentence was lost in a gasp of air as she was flipped onto her back. All Bec saw was a pair of molten emerald eyes before the T-shirt she was wearing was yanked over her head and Luke was all but attacking her breasts.

He sucked one nipple into his mouth, drawing on it in almost desperate pulls. His other hand was on her stomach, her hip, in between her thighs, delving into the liquid heat of her.

And he was ruthless.

Thumb pressing against her clit, rubbing in firm circles that had her crying out his name. But he didn't stop, just switched breasts and kept the rhythm of his thumb constant as he slipped one thick finger inside her.

Bec gasped, hips flying up, desperate for more than that minimal intrusion.

She wanted him pushing home, filling her to excess, the burn of his thick length mixing with her desire until she was engulfed in flames of pleasure.

"Luke—" He stole the rest of her words with a kiss, fingers continuing to work as his free hand angled her head and he replicated the rhythm of his thumb with his tongue in her mouth.

She couldn't breathe. Every muscle in her body was taut and coiled, desperate for release.

"I . . . Luke . . . *Oh God.* I need—"

He slipped another finger into her, pressed firmly on her clit.

And implosion.

Stars behind her eyes, pleasure radiating out from her core, spilling into her limbs, making them heavy and lax.

Nothing.

She felt nothing but those waves of bliss, and it could have been thirty seconds or a minute or an eternity before they slowed and finally, finally she was able to wrench back her eyelids and look up at the only man who'd ever held any power over her.

"You're beautiful," he murmured.

Her lips curved. "Condom. Nightstand. Now."

She'd almost expected Luke to laugh at her caveman instructions, but instead of teasing her, his eyes went somehow hotter. "You sure? I don't want to hurt—"

Bec reached down and gripped the hard length of him, loving the way his head fell forward and his hips thrust toward her. "I need you, baby," she murmured, knowing that the reassuring words came from some place inside her that only Luke had access to. "Please, come inside me."

One long look.

One hard swallow.

Then he reached over her left shoulder and extracted a condom from the nightstand. A few seconds later he'd rolled it on, was staring down at her with anticipation and worry and—

Bec pulled his head down to hers, kissing him this time, thrusting *her* tongue into his mouth for a change. She hitched a leg around his hips, lifting off the bed, bringing herself close enough to rub against the hard length of his cock. They both caught their breath, and she moaned into his mouth at the feel of hard gliding through silky folds, of hot meeting wet, of—

She tightened her leg, sinking back down to the mattress and bringing him on top of her. Chest against chest, hips against hips, hard against soft.

"Becky," he groaned as she wrapped her other leg around him.

"Mmm." She changed the angle of her pelvis, catching the

tip of his erection at her opening, teasing them both by allowing just the slightest bit of him inside her.

The smallest dip before retreating. Another dip. *Another.* Until she felt sweat break out on Luke's back, until she couldn't take it anymore. Until *he* couldn't either.

She shifted just as he drove home.

"Fuck," she hissed, eyes going wide, lips parting.

He paused, worry written in the lines of his face. "Shit, sorry. I—"

"No." Legs tightening around his waist, she pulled him closer. "Do that again."

He slid out, pressed back in.

Hard and deep and not particularly finessed, he drove into her. And fuck, but it was the best ever. Raw and hot, shooting her up the precipice and straight over the edge.

She screamed, actually screamed as she came, and her sore throat would serve as a testament to that later.

He pushed once, twice more, before calling out her name.

"Becky!"

In that moment, heart racing, lungs sawing, and pleasure coursing through her limp body, Luke still somehow found the energy to cradle her like she was the most precious object in the universe. The only man she'd ever loved was next to her, and she found she didn't even care that he hadn't called her Bec.

Becky.

She could live with that.

At least it wasn't sugar pie.

Her lips twitched, her eyes shut, and she forgot all about the pressing matters at work. She just cuddled closer and soaked in Luke Pearson.

Yeah, she could live with that.

SEVENTEEN

Luke

"NO," he said to his group back in Texas, interrupting the presentation they'd been videoconferencing. "That's not the right strategy. Come on, guys, this is basic science. If you roll all the variables out at once, you won't be able to pinpoint cause and effect."

The table turned to look at the camera, at him.

Years ago that would have made him uncomfortable.

Now, Luke didn't mind stepping up and being the leader they needed. In fact, he found he thrived under the pressure.

"I didn't think of it that way," Trevor, one of his leads in the R&D department at Pearson Energy said.

"*Think* about it," Luke told him before turning his attention to the rest of the room. "We have a chance at something good here, guys. The product is great, yes, but there are flaws that need to be worked out before it goes to market. That's what the site here will bring us—existing infrastructure to tie into, a huge grid to practice on." He thrust a hand through his hair. "We play this right, and this technology will be big. We fuck up, and—"

He didn't need to elaborate.

The project would crash and burn before it got anywhere.

And the years of effort, research, testing? They would be for naught.

"Go back to the drawing board," he said. "We'll discuss next week."

He clicked off and sighed, shutting off his laptop before pulling out his phone to go through his ever-filling inbox.

"You're sexy when you give orders."

Luke turned, not having heard Becky come in. It had been a week since that night—the best sleep of his life, followed up by the best *sex* of his life—and his *sugar pie* had graciously offered him the use of her apartment.

"*You already know the codes anyway,*" she'd told him.

Not being a stupid man, or not *all* the time anyway, Luke had readily agreed.

No more hotel.

No more pitying looks from the maids.

Just Becky and trying to get her naked at every opportunity.

He pushed to his feet, crossed over to her, and took her into his arms. His heart pulsed, just like it did every time she allowed him to do it.

"I missed you," he said and kissed her.

"You're just trying to bribe your way into knowing what my date is," she said when they broke apart.

"I'm trying to bribe my way into *something*," he agreed, slipping his hands down and gripping the lush curves of her ass. She was wearing a black pencil skirt and fuck, did it drive him crazy with the urge to tug it up, bend her over and—

Becky stepped away from him. Started unbuttoning her cream blouse.

It hit the carpet silently.

White lace. *See-through* white lace.

"What—?"

She turned her back on him, reached up to tug down the gold zipper that held her skirt together. Slowly. So *fucking* slowly it slid down, exposing porcelain skin bisected by the tiniest white thong Luke had ever seen.

A shimmy of her hips, black fabric sliding down thighs he was desperate to get his mouth between.

The skirt hit the floor.

He was hard and aching, but watching the slow lift of one black stiletto-clad foot stepping out of that crumpled piece of clothing followed by the other, made him even hotter.

Her ass. *Fuck* her ass.

Two perfect globes that jiggled just the slightest bit as she moved. Fucking perfection. But then Luke almost swallowed his tongue when she bent to pick up the skirt and glanced back at him over her shoulder.

The pink tip of her tongue darted out, moistened her bottom lip.

"While I did enjoy playing mini-golf with you Saturday night," she said, straightening and tossing the skirt onto her couch, "I was thinking that date five could be a little more . . ." One blonde brow lifted as she waited.

His words sounded like gravel. "A little more what?"

"More sex," she stage-whispered.

His dick pulsed, threatening to tear through his zipper.

Becky closed the distance between them, cupped him through his jeans. "I'm horny and wet, and I want you, Pearson." She rose on tiptoe, whispered in his ear. "Dinner on the pier can wait."

He had enough presence of mind to file her date preference away to remember later before she undid his zipper and dropped to her knees.

"Sweetheart," he began. "You don't have—"

She tugged and his cock sprung free from his boxer briefs. Then her mouth was on him, tongue tracing the hard length of him, hand moving up and down in a rhythm that had his knees shaking and his eyes rolling back into his head.

Fingers clenching into fists at his sides, Luke focused on not immediately blowing his load.

But *fuck* it felt good.

Her mouth was hot and wet, her tongue teased the underside of him, and her hand gripped him tightly as she stroked him straight to insanity.

"Mmm." She moaned, taking him deeper.

Then she did something with her tongue that made his vision go black.

And then she did it again.

"Enough," he growled, gripping her by her shoulders and yanking her up. He toed off his shoes, yanked a condom out of the back pocket of his jeans, and rolled it on.

In one movement, he lifted Becky up into his arms and turned to pin her against the wall.

"Lu—"

Rip. Her underwear flew over his shoulder, but he didn't look to see where it landed. Instead, he shifted so he was in between Becky's thighs and pushed into her.

"*Oh*," Becky gasped.

"*Fuuck*," he groaned.

Pictures rattled as he set a pounding rhythm. It was too much, too fast. He was rushing, needed to slow down. A framed print of something crashed to the ground and, worried he was too out of control, that he was going to hurt her, Luke forced himself to slow.

"*No*," she said, and her fingers dug into his nape, her legs wrapped tighter around his waist. "Don't stop. Please, *God*, don't stop."

And fuck if he could deny her that.

Not when he was riding the razor's edge already. Not when his control was all but eroded. Not when she was tight and wet and felt so fucking good clamping around him.

Thud. Thud. *Thud.*

More pictures hit the floor.

Thank God Becky's apartment was the penthouse and they were alone on this floor. But the neighbors below were going to be pissed.

Luke couldn't bring himself to care.

He kept up the rapid pace, shifting his hold so it was his hands taking the pounding rather than Becky's spine.

"Yes. Please," she said, pressing against him. "*Yes.* Oh *fuck.*"

And then she exploded.

One. Two strokes and he followed her over.

He came to sitting bare-assed on the hardwood floor with Becky in his lap.

Holy shit. Holy *fucking* shit.

"How long have we been like this?" she asked, laziness in every syllable.

Luke shook his head. "Fuck, if I know." He surveyed the damage around them, only one picture remained on the wall, the rest were scattered on the hardwood floor. Luckily, they must not have had glass in the frames, otherwise his ass would be sushi and he'd much rather *eat* sushi than have his ass masquerade as it.

"We should get up." Becky started to push out of his lap, then sighed and snuggled closer.

"I'll get us to bed," he said, wrapping his arms around her.

A good minute passed.

"Are we moving?" she asked.

He chuckled. "As soon as I can feel my legs."

Her breath was warm on his neck as she laughed. "God, I love you," she said. "Let's just stay like this forever."

And if Luke's heart hadn't already been branded with Becky's name, this moment would have burned the mark right onto it.

EIGHTEEN

Bec

SOMEHOW, Luke had managed to get them into her bed, which was a good thing because Bec knew there was no way she could have gotten there on her own.

She'd been content to curl up in the living room, Luke as her personal blanket.

But this was just as good, naked limbs intertwined, his hand snug around her waist. It was just the other thing, the reason why she hadn't felt like going out that evening.

The Phone Call.

Yes, it deserved capital letters.

Because her father had called her.

And another one of the boxes she had carefully contained in her heart, locked up and wound with barbed wire, preventing pesky feelings from escaping, had ruptured.

He'd disappointed her so much.

And he'd called.

Bec had let the call go to voicemail, not wanting to talk to the man who'd shipped her off when she'd needed him the most. She'd reached out to him so many damned times and . . .

Brick wall.

Like father, like daughter.

"What's wrong?" Luke asked into the silence.

She didn't ask how he knew to ask, was just glad that he *did* ask. And where in the past she would have brushed him off, just internalized the tangle of emotions she was feeling over the fact her father had called, today she told Luke what happened.

"My dad called me today."

He never called.

Ever.

She was *always* the one to reach out.

And the fact that he had? It terrified her. Would she turn back into that pathetic creature, striving, doing everything in her power for his approval?

Or was he sick? The thought of losing him hurt, despite everything he'd done.

But maybe he just . . . needed her? For the first time ever, maybe her father needed her or wanted to spend time with her or—

That hope was hard to stifle, especially because she knew better than to allow herself to feel hopeful when disappointment was the more likely outcome of interacting with her father.

Luke brushed a hand down her arm. "What'd he have to say?"

"I don't know."

He rose up on one elbow, rotating so he could glance down at her. And not speak, apparently, because all he did was stare at her. Then lifted one brown brow.

Bec sighed. "Don't look at me like that."

The brow went higher. "Like what?"

"Like you're all . . . I don't know, not judgy exactly, but disapproving."

"Becky, sweetheart—"

"Don't sweetheart me."

"Becky, then." He paused, giving her a chance to insert another protest, but between getting so damned used to him and her friends calling her Becky over the last few weeks and feeling so unsettled by her father's call, she couldn't even drum up a correction. "It's not like you to avoid things."

She scoffed. "I spent ten years avoiding *you*."

A smile tugged at the corners of his mouth. "Should we call it a case of mutual avoidance?"

"Sure." A begrudging agreement.

Her eyes drifted around her bedroom, deliberately avoiding his gaze as she took in the pale blue walls. Her linens were crisp white cotton because she'd always loved the way hotel sheets felt and had wanted to replicate that, but aside from one print of a Scottish seascape that CeCe had painted for her, the room was almost empty of personality.

Or empty of her personality anyway.

Even the living room and kitchen were mostly bare of knick-knacks, the only items hanging on the walls pictures of her and her friends or things the Sextant had brought back for her— more drawings from CeCe, who always teased when presenting her with original artwork by saying Bec was the only one of the group who actually had wall space to spare; a fern leaf encased in amber from Rachel, who'd visited New Zealand with her other half, Sebastian; a pencil sketch of Berlin from Heather; pictures of Bec with Abby's kids.

Bec hadn't printed the photos or framed them or even hung them on the walls.

That had all been the girls. Two months ago, they'd bullied her into running to Target for hooks and frames, and they all had spent an entire evening hanging them up in her apartment . . . and also drinking wine.

Which had resulted in a few crooked pictures. But Bec couldn't bring herself to straighten them, even after they'd gone.

Her friends had hung them for her.

Her friends had given her a gift she'd never known she wanted.

A home.

Oh, she'd long used the convenient excuse of being too busy with work, of insane hours being the reason her apartment was sterile and barely lived in. She was hardly home as it was, why bother investing any time into decorating somewhere that she spent so little time in?

But work wasn't the issue.

Not really.

It was just easier to pretend it *was* work rather than to admit the truth. Because the truth was that *she* was the one with the problem.

Why create a home when it would just be torn away from her?

"Talk to me, sweetheart."

She shook her head, blinking back tears. "I j-just . . ." She sniffed. "Dammit. I never realized how much I was missing out on until you came back."

"What do you mean?"

And so she told him everything.

Not the bare facts of losing her mom, of moving, of boarding school.

But how after her mom had died, her dad didn't come home. He didn't explain what happened. No, that dubious honor had gone to the person he'd hired to watch her while their family home was packed away and sold, any happy memories being regulated into the back of her mind.

"I lost my dad then too. He was working all the time and when he was home, he couldn't stand the sight of me." She let Luke hug her tight. "He'd disengaged, become cold and unfeeling when I needed him the most. He hired people to take me to school, to feed me, to comfort me if I had a nightmare."

"Oh, sweetheart."

Tears burned but she blinked them back. "I just thought if I could be smart enough, good enough, pretty enough that maybe he'd notice—" She shook her head. "Folly. All of it. Because I had to find that worth in myself and it took me damn near twenty years."

"But . . ." He hesitated, but she nodded, encouraging him to ask. They were baring it all, baby. Full-on honest fucking communication.

If he saw this part of her and left—

Luke opened his mouth, closed it, then hugged her again. "I can see it in your eyes."

"What?" It was a stiff question.

"You think this will make me run."

Well, yeah.

She couldn't even get her own father to stay.

"I'm not leaving," he said. "What I was going to ask is why you didn't tell me all of this before. You made it seem—"

"Like it was no big deal."

"Yeah."

Bec blew out a breath. "Don't you see? It *had* to be no big deal or I wouldn't have survived. I wouldn't have been able to cope with my father moving back to California and leaving me in New York. I couldn't have dealt with him not visiting, or flying me home over vacation." Her voice dropped. "It was easier to just pretend it was me."

"Then me."

She blinked. "Yeah." They'd created something that had

resembled a home . . . or at least, the only sort of home she knew how to create, and that hadn't exactly gone well. "I learned it was easier to put a very specific distance between myself and the rest of the world. It was safer."

"Sweetheart, I'm so sorry."

"It's okay. I'm—I had Abby and Sera."

They were the only real caveat to her plans for distance. They'd barreled on through any walls, merrily leading new—and wonderful—women along with them. And Bec? Well, she'd started to feel a bit like the Grinch, her frosty exterior hiding a heart with the potential for growth on the inside.

Now was that a millennial description of a classic children's book or what?

Fingertips brushed her bottom lip. "Why are you smiling when you're so sad here"—he touched the spot over her heart then one temple—"and here?"

"I am sad, but I realized that I have my friends, that I have you and that makes things hurt a little less." She sighed, smile fading. "I don't know why my Dad called because I didn't pick up. I haven't listened to the message. I didn't—I don't know if I even want to open that old wound back up."

Luke sank back down to the mattress, pulling her so she was tucked against his side then slowly running his fingers through her hair. "That's why you jumped me first thing when you got home?"

Home. There was that word again.

But the smugness in his tone also meant that she retained a little Darden spirit. She tugged at his chest hair, mock-glaring at the yummy expanse of muscle. "*You* jumped *me*, if I recall. *I* was just trying to give *you* a nice—"

He tickled her side, cutting off her self-righteous rant by inducing giggles. "Dropping to your knees in front of a man tends to get you jumped." She glanced up, laughing harder when she saw he was staring down at her and waggling his brows.

"See if that happens again," she muttered when she finally regained control of herself. "Not likely."

"Brutal."

"Damn straight."

He kissed the top of her head. "Tough. Beautiful. Smart. Sexy. Funny—"

"What are you doing?"

"Brilliant. Valuable. Worthy. Clever. *Sassy*," he continued, staring down at her as though just reciting character traits was a normal part of human conversation.

"I—"

Fingers covered her lips. "You're all of those things, sweetheart, and so many more. Loving. Independent. Sweet. Vulnerable. Courageous. Resilient—"

"Stop," she said. "Please, Luke. I'm not all of those things. I barely hold it together most of the time."

"And welcome to the rest of the world, Becky. So many of us are just treading water." He cupped her cheek. "But you. *You* are special. You're so much more than a grieving daughter or a ridiculously smart lawyer. You're more than just a friend or girlfriend or lover. You're—"

"Do not say special."

"Tough shit, Rebecca." He cupped the other cheek, waited until her eyes were locked with his. "Tough shit because you *are* special."

"Oh, *fuck*," she murmured.

Because her eyes burned and her throat was tight and, dammit, there were those little drops of salty liquid leaking out of the corners of her lashes. They dripped down her cheeks, pooling on Luke's chest.

He wrapped her in his arms, held her tight. "You're allowed

to cry," he said. "You're allowed to feel. You're allowed to be torn up because as much as you don't want to admit it, the wound your father inflicted on your heart isn't healed."

"Fuck off," she snapped. "I'm fine. I don't need—I'm not some broken thing."

"Of course you're not," he said, his tone soft despite her harshness. "But Becky, sweetheart, you're *human*. And that means that your feelings won't always stay collated into nice, neat files. Sometimes shit spills out and things get messy."

She pushed against his chest, but Luke wouldn't let her go.

And then *she* couldn't let him go.

She hadn't been allowed emotions. Not for so fucking long.

No. The reality was that she hadn't allowed *herself* to feel.

Because down that path came disappointment.

Warm palms brushed over her hair, glided along her spine, slow, gentle movements that soothed her as she cried and cried and cried. Tears for her mom, for her father, and Luke, and . . . for her.

She couldn't ever remember crying for her own losses, though she must have at some point.

Bec remembered her mother's funeral, how there had been two caskets, one for her mom and one for her brother, Liam. She remembered seeing the wooden letters she'd picked out on a shopping trip with her mother. They'd been displayed in front of his tiny casket, and she'd grabbed the L, desperate to have something tangible of her mother and the baby when everything in life seemed so fragile and transient.

Her father had torn it from her hands at the gravesite, tossed it down into the hole.

She shivered at the memory of its thud hitting the top of the casket.

And yet, Bec hadn't cried. She'd understood that it was her job to be strong for her father, to be tough and resilient and—

She shouldn't have had to be any of those things.

Not at seven.

Not at ten.

Not as a child.

And it made her so fucking heartbroken that'd she'd needed to be that way just because her father hadn't been able to put aside his grief enough to love her as she should have been loved.

She was livid. So fucking angry that he'd forced her into that and that he'd reached out *now?* After years of ignoring emails and texts and voicemails, after only occasionally deeming her worthy of the rare one-sentence but incredibly terse reply. After everything, he wanted to speak with her now.

Where in the fuck did he get off?

Bec's shoulders went tight as a sudden thought occurred to her.

Luke's hand stopped its soothing movement. "What is it?"

"What if . . ." She shook her head. "It's stupid that I assumed this whole thing has to do with some big behavioral or physical change of his. It's been more than twenty years, he's—" She broke off, inhaled and exhaled deeply. "Just because *I've* changed doesn't mean that he's going to be any different. He's probably just wishing me an early birthday."

Except her birthday wasn't for another month.

He'd also never called her on or near her birthday before.

This was different. She knew that as instinctively as she knew when to take on a particularly challenging case.

"You don't believe that," Luke said after a moment.

"No," she said, her voice soft, her fingers trailing over his chest, tracing nonsensical patterns on his skin that somehow soothed her. "No," she repeated. "I don't believe that. He called for a reason. One I don't know or can't fathom, but something has changed."

"He's getting older," Luke said. "He might want—"

"Don't."

Don't get her hopes up.

Don't make her feel something when she wasn't sure she could ever forgive her father.

"Okay," he said, fingers slipping through her hair again, petting her, *gentling* her.

They lay like that for a long time, their bodies intertwined, Luke's hands moving over her body, and that comforting touch had the tension leeching out of her.

"There's only one way to find out what your father really wants," he eventually murmured.

Bec sucked in a breath, knowing what was coming but still having to ask anyway. "How?"

"You listen to the voicemail."

Damn. She'd been afraid he'd say that.

NINETEEN

Luke

HE WATCHED the change wash over Becky.

Her shoulders stiffened, the arm that had formerly laid pliant across his chest tightened, her breathing sped, and . . . then all that tension dissipated.

"You had to go and say it, didn't you?" Forced lightness laced her tone. "I was happy to pretend to be too busy, to *forget* the message was there, and then you had to be all reasonable."

Luke chuckled. "Sorry, not sorry?"

"Hmph."

"You know I'm right," he told her. "You *hate* that I'm right, but it doesn't change the fact that I'm—"

"Right?" She pushed up to sitting. "Why don't you say it a few more times?"

His lips curved and, not deterred by the sass in the least, he tugged her back down to his side. "I'm so right. Gloriously, perfectly right—"

Her hand clamped over his mouth. "Yes, yes. Now you don't have to rub—"

He flicked his tongue out, teasing the sensitive skin on her palm. Becky jumped and tugged her hand away. "Really, Pearson?"

Luke folded his arms behind his head. "Let's continue with how I'm right."

"Ugh." She started to get off the bed. "No," she grumbled. "I've had enough of that—*ack!*" He'd snagged her wrist, yanking her to the mattress, and climbing on top of her. She was naked, a fact his body definitely noticed, but she was also running, so he focused on the more pressing issues first.

"Listen to the message, sugar pie." He bent his head, sucked one nipple in his mouth.

"*Luke!*"

"Do it," he said, kissing his way down her body. Becky's hands wove into his hair and pushed ever so discretely in the direction of her pussy. He dragged his mouth lower, brushed his tongue along the insides of her thighs. "Do it, and I'll do that thing with my fingers again."

She stilled, lifted her head up to look at him. "*Really?*"

He circled her clit with his thumb. "Really."

"I can't believe you're talking about my vagina and my father in the same sentence."

Slow circles. Gentle, teasing circles.

"Technically, I didn't put those two things together."

"You im—implied it."

"*You* inferred it." He spread her wide, bent to suck her clit into his mouth.

"*Fuck.*" Her hips jumped, her fingers went tight against his scalp, and his dick, already hard and aching, turned to granite. As usual, things with his Becky had escalated further than he'd intended. "Stop using big words," she said. "You know it turns me on."

Luke's eyes shot to hers, and he saw the mischief in those gray pools. "Stop equivocating and just listen to the message."

"Mmm. *Equivocating.*" Her head flopped back to the mattress. "So. Many. Letters."

"You're such a—" Fuck he couldn't think of another big word, not when he was between Becky's thighs, the salty tang of her against his tongue. *There.* Got one. "Such a hedonist."

She laughed. "Oh, my God," she said. "We're absolutely ridiculous."

"I'm the one trying to lick your pussy here." He circled her clit with his tongue.

"No, what you're *trying—ah—*to do is oral sex me into submission."

He paused. "Is it working?"

Laughter shook her frame, tightened her legs around him. "Yes, Pearson. It's working. Stop teasing and make me come, and I'll listen to the voicemail."

A flick of his tongue made her moan. "I understand where we went wrong now." He slid one finger through her folds, pushed it inside. "Before," he said as her breath caught and her hips tilted, trying to get him deeper.

"What the fuck are you talking about?" she snapped. "I—*oh fuck.*"

He'd done the thing with his finger.

"I should have sexed you into submission."

Hazy eyes met his. "Never would have worked."

He repeated the thing with his finger, watching as her eyes rolled to the back of her head. "If I'd known this"—more finger—"it would have worked."

"You—*ah*—act like knowing how to find a woman's G-spot should earn you a gold medal."

"I don't give a fuck about medals, so long as *this*"—another teasing touch—"has you screaming my name."

Her mouth dropped open. "Oh, *damn*. You're good, Pearson."

He grinned.

"Fine." She lifted her hips slightly. "Sex me into submission, and *then* I'll listen to the voicemail."

"I thought you'd never ask."

"Men are such—" she huffed, but her complaint was cut off when she cried out his name.

Yup. Luke definitely deserved that gold medal.

AFTERWARD, they showered, threw on the bare minimum of clothes, then found their way back to Becky's bed.

He picked up her cell from her nightstand. "Ready?"

"No," she muttered, but took it from him anyway, punching in four numbers to unlock the screen. They corresponded to a date in the past he was hoping to replicate at some point—four ten—the day he'd first proposed to her.

She hadn't accepted . . . because that wasn't his Becky.

She would never be an easy woman to love. She was formed of layers and layers, some soft and generous, some vulnerable and protected by sharp spikes, but if he could make his way to the core of her again?

That was the best.

If someone made it into that inner circle, his Becky loved without barriers. She would move the world to make that person happy, love them at the expense of herself.

She gave everything. He just hadn't been able to give everything back.

But he was different now. She owned him and he would give her everything down to his last breath.

Her finger hovered over the button to play the message for a moment. "I—"

"You got this."

Eyes locked with his, the finger came down, and the voice-mail began to play.

"Hi, uh, Rebecca. My name is Helen. I'm your father's . . . um, wife. I—"

A loud gust of air made them both wince.

"I'm sorry. I probably shouldn't be calling. I know you don't want to hear from us, but your father is sick and . . . I, uh, thought you should know in case. Anyway, I hope you'll come. He'd really like to see you . . ."

Helen rattled off the name of the hospital and a room number.

The message ended, and she played it again. Then a third time. But when she would have gone for a fourth, Luke stayed her hands.

She didn't fight him, just let him slip her cell from her grip and set it on the nightstand.

"He—" Her shoulders sagged the slightest bit. "He didn't tell me he'd gotten remarried." Her voice was small, too fucking small for the vibrant woman he loved. "I've talked to him once a year on his birthday. I've emailed. Texted. And this Helen thinks —" She shook her head, hands clenching into fists where they rested on the outsides of her thighs. "I *waited* for him to call me, hoped he'd remember my birthday or maybe send me a fucking Christmas present." She jumped to her feet, paced alongside the bed. "Do you know that before Abby and Sera, I was the *only* one who spent every holiday at school? *Alone.* I was so pathetic that the different teachers took turns bringing me home so I wouldn't be by myself. And he—*he* has the fucking gall to say that it was me? That I didn't want to talk to him. I—I—"

She stumbled to a stop, knees giving out.

But he was there before she crumpled to the floor.

Luke scooped her into his arms, carried her back to bed, and held her as his powerful, strong, courageous woman lost her battle with tears.

Sometimes the creatures with the hardest shells had the softest insides.

And his Becky, she had a really hard shell.

TWENTY

Bec

SHE'D BEEN CATEGORIZING Luke in her head as the man she'd loved.

Emphasis on the past tense.

But as she looked around the living room of her apartment, the members of the Sextant who were in town gathered because of the man she loved *today*.

Luke had called them while she'd slept off her crying fit, and now it was after ten and her friends all had to work the next day and they'd still come and . . . great. Because the fact that they'd come, that Heather had FaceTimed in the middle of her workday in Berlin, that CeCe was on a beach in the Mediterranean and still had called made her feel like crying all over again.

"I don't like having feelings," she muttered.

Abby shoved a tissue box at her. "You're not the Tin Man. You've always had a big heart, *Becky*."

Bec narrowed her eyes at her friend, who just grinned unrepentantly, then turned to glare at Luke, who raised his hands in surrender and mouthed, *"I didn't know."*

"Why do you think you're usually the first one any of us call when we're in trouble, huh?"

"Because I'm single and nearby?"

Luke snorted and slipped into the kitchen, abandoning her, the jerk.

"Except, you probably have the heaviest workload of all of us, Heather aside," Rachel said.

"More," Heather chimed in. "Clay has made me slow down the last six months."

Sera's lips twitched. "What exactly is your definition of slowing down?"

"Not beach time," CeCe said, reclining back on her lounger and taking a sip of a colorful drink with a purple umbrella in it.

"Or staying in the same time zone for more than a few days at a time," Rachel teased.

Heather glared. "Considering you're the one who makes my schedule, whose fault is that?"

"Ladies," Abby said. "We've been called here for a reason."

Exactly one moment of silence before the room burst into laughter, including Bec.

"We've . . . been called . . ." Sera was bent over on the couch, clutching her side as giggles erupted out of her.

"We need cloaks," Rachel managed between laughs.

"And a boiling cauldron," CeCe added.

"Magic crystals." Heather.

"More wine," Bec said.

"Amen to that, sister," Abby muttered. "I swear, you guys, I don't even know why we're friends sometimes."

Sera tugged their reluctant friend into a hug. "Aw! You love us."

Luke walked in with a bottle of wine and filled their glasses, then sat down on the couch next to Bec. "Should I go?" he whispered. "I don't want to leave you, but I also don't want to intrude if you want to be with the girls—"

This man.

God, she loved him.

"Thank you." She cupped his cheek. "For caring. I'd like it if you stayed, at least until any talk of penises starts happening."

His brows rose. "Is that going to happen?"

Her lips twitched. "Guaranteed."

He pressed a kiss to her forehead. "Okay. Staying till talk of penises commences."

Abby waggled her brows. "So tempting."

"Shut it, you," Bec told her.

"What happened to the picture of the kiddos?" Abby asked innocently.

Bec's eyes narrowed at her friend. Luke had picked up the pictures they'd knocked to the ground before her friends had come over, and though Sera had given the naked walls a second look, no one had said anything.

Abby grinned unrepentantly.

"Becky—*Bec* is considering redecorating," Luke said.

Smiles all around, the punks. But then Sera sighed. "You've got a good one there."

Bec's mouth curved. "I do," she said. "I really do. Don't know why he puts up with me, considering I've spent this entire evening pretending to be a gigantic pile of tears."

"Well, first," Abby said. "He's lucky you let him come back into your life—no offense, Luke."

"None taken," he said with a grin. "I am lucky she decided to give me another chance."

"Second, you're fucking awesome, dude." She leaned over Sera and lightly punched Bec's arm. "What happened to the

Rebecca Darden, kickass lawyer who doesn't take any shit from anyone?"

"She got motherfucking feelings," Bec grumbled. "It sucks ass."

"I happen to like your ass," Luke said.

"I bet he does," Heather said with a cackle. "What kinds of things is he doing with that yummy ass, *Becky?*"

Bec stood, grabbed Luke's hand and tugged him to his feet as well. "And that's your cue."

He hesitated. "But there wasn't any talk of penises."

And now all the girls were cackling.

"There was yummy ass talk," Bec told him. "That's close enough."

Luke's lips were tugging up at the corners. "If you say so." He leaned in, pressed his lips to the spot just in front of her ear. "You sure you're okay?"

Bec nodded. "I am."

He rolled back on his heels. "Okay then, I'm going on an ice cream run. Orders?" he asked the room at large, typing the requests into his phone and chuckling when Heather and CeCe expressed their jealousy at missing out. After they'd all finished, he leaned in and kissed her soundly on the lips and long enough to make her head spin. "I'll be back in a bit." He started to leave, paused, and met her gaze. "I love you."

"Dude," CeCe breathed after he'd gone. "You need to put a ring on that."

They all laughed, and then Heather said, "As much as I'm enjoying this little tête-à-tête, I have a meeting in fifteen minutes and don't want to miss all the important juicy bits."

"*Juicy* bits?" Abby said with a snort.

"Yes," Heather replied. "Big ol' giant juicy bits. I like them. I want them—"

"I'm going to puke," Rachel interjected.

Sera nodded. "Let's step away from juicy bits and move onto emotions."

"I second that," CeCe said.

"I'm still semi-interested in Heather's juicy bits—" Bec stopped, made a face. "Okay, that sounded a lot less dirty in my head. I'm sorry to everyone involved."

"Bec." Sera took her hand. "For the love of God, please save us more juice talk and get to the point."

Bec took a glug from her wine glass. "My dad, or rather, my *stepmother* called me."

Silence. Only half the room—herself, Abby, and Sera—knew why that was such a big deal, and so Abby and Sera were stunned into muteness by the news. Rachel, CeCe, and Heather were quiet, as they no doubt waited for more information as to why her stepmother calling was such a big deal.

"The long and short of it," she said, "is that my mom died, and my dad shipped me off to boarding school. I was the *Harry Potter* equivalent of not going home for holidays, of being lonely and isolated, except my dad was still alive. He didn't visit or call, not even on my birthday. Every bit of contact we've had over the last twenty-something years has been because of me, because I called."

She sighed, took another sip of wine. "And even then, even after I moved back, he still never had time to meet for lunch or dinner, never wanted me to come by his house or office. Turns out he remarried and never mentioned it to me, then started another life, and other than my trust fund—which I haven't touched since I graduated from law school—he hasn't given me a second thought."

Yay for family.

Another sip from her glass as clarity dawned. "I think I reminded him too much of my mom, of everything he lost. Maybe I should have pushed harder, called more—"

"What. A. Dick." Harsh words from a source Bec wouldn't have expected.

From CeCe.

"You needed him, and he abandoned you. Good parents are good because they put their kids first." Her tone took on a bitter note. "I know because mine didn't."

"We're all on that particular train, CeCe," Heather said. "I had parents who made babies like they were going out of style but didn't want to actually spend time with them. Abby's parents are no peaches—her mom having an affair and, no offense, but your bio dad is a total dickwad—"

"None taken," Abby said.

"Let's see," Heather tapped her chin. "CeCe's disowned her because, *gasp*, she wanted to live her own life. Rachel's dad was both absentee and shockingly bad. Who's left?"

Sera raised her hand. "I don't have any of that. My parents are still happily married. But I am incredibly sorry you guys went through that."

"Girl," Abby touched her arm. "Your parents aren't peaches, either. Remember when you wanted to stop with the pageants, and they shipped you off to boarding school? Or the time you didn't want to be in that commercial, so they forbid you from eating anything except for carrots and spinach until you agreed?"

"It wasn't that bad. I was getting chunky—"

Heather raised a brow. "You'd what? Gone from a size double zero to a zero?"

"I—" Sera fumbled for a few moments to find the right words then sighed. "Okay, fine. My parents *were* pretty shitty."

"Glad you got there in the end," Heather said with a smirk. "But putting that revelation aside, my point is that none of us are the same, aside from our dirty ass minds—"

Abby snorted, thus confirming *her* dirty-minded tendencies.

Heather ignored her. "We're all very different and *still* not one of us had stellar parents. And at the risk of digressing, but something I think is also important is that the common experience of going through that is probably why we found each other in the first place. Like knows like. Pain knows pain." Heather waved a hand, probably because she was bordering on poetic, and Heather definitely didn't do poetic. "Anyway, I think the most important thing we can deduce is that their ineptitude has nothing to do with us."

Bec frowned, and she wasn't the only one in the room to do so, but Heather went on with her explanation before they could question her logic.

"I'm not saying any of us are perfect. Far from it, actually. I'm just saying our imperfection and, on the opposite side, our success and whatever happiness we've managed to carve out in our lives haven't happened because of them. We've managed to become the people we are today *in spite* of their interference and absence and general douchebaggery."

Abby nodded. "My dad definitely has a degree in douchebaggery."

"And mine," CeCe added.

"Ditto," Rachel said.

"I guess it's no wonder why we're so fucked up," Bec said dryly, and they all laughed. "Heather, I know you have to go, and I definitely feel what you're saying. But . . . I guess I don't necessarily feel comfortable blaming a sick man for my emotional problems. I've never been one to not take responsibility for my actions."

"Which makes you a much better person than your father."

Oh.

Bec's heart twisted. Not because she believed that she was the better person, but because she'd always blamed herself for her dad leaving her.

It was her fault that he'd gone.

She'd seen the pictures, knew she looked like her mother, knew she reminded him too much of her mom and that the resemblance hurt him.

But that was . . . bullshit.

It wasn't *her* fault.

And it never had been.

Strange how just thinking the words changed everything, as though a switch had flipped in her brain or maybe in her heart, or maybe Luke and her friends had finally given her the courage to understand.

She'd been a kid.

It wasn't on her.

Bec blinked back tears, though instead of crying for her past and the hurt and the painful memories, those tears were full of relief.

Relief she no longer had to carry that burden.

Relief her life no longer had to be defined by something that had happened to her growing up.

Relief she finally could be herself and that she didn't always need to be tough or impenetrable or unfeeling.

Arms wrapped around her, holding tightly as she sniffed. "Okay, fine. You win. You guys are the best," she said.

"Of course we are," Heather joked, startling a laugh out of her.

Sera broke away from the group hug. "So great, Ms. Becky here doesn't have to see her dad. She can just move on with Luke and live happily ever after."

"No." This time the rebuttal was from Bec herself. "I'm going to see my father because I have balls of steel. I'm going to clear that final hurdle and put this shit behind me. *Then* I'm going to move on with my HEA with Luke."

"Damn," Sera whispered. "You're good."

"Not exactly," Bec told her. "I just know I have to be done with this once and for all."

On the screen, Heather waved a hand—in *these are not the droids you're looking for* fashion. "I've trained you well, young Jedi." Her lips twitched. "I'm sorry that I need to run, but—"

"Go," Bec told her. "And thank you." Heather's portion of the screen went blank, and Bec looked around the room. "Thank you all. I couldn't have done this, be semi-healthy and happy without you guys. I'd still be in the office working fourteen-hour days and not enjoying anything other than the occasional book and girls' night."

"Now you're down to ten-hour days," Sera teased. "That's huge progress."

For her it was, but she also understood Sera's point. "I'm not stopping here. I'm going to grab onto my happy ending, and I'm going to fight for it and I'm never letting it go again."

"Damn straight you are," Abby said with a nod.

Rachel lifted her palm for a high five. "Fuck yeah, *Becky*."

"Give him hell, *sugar pie*," CeCe chimed in.

"I take it back. I hate you all," Bec muttered.

"I'll get more wine," Sera crowed. "And then we're talking about how Rachel and Sebastian got caught making out in Heather's office."

Rachel's cheeks went fluorescent, and Bec grinned.

God, she loved these woman.

Then Luke pushed through the front door, individual cartons of ice cream in a bag that he doled out to each one of them in turn, like some sexy, sweet treat bearing Santa Claus, and Bec's cheeks actually hurt from smiling so much.

Because she fucking loved that man, too.

TWENTY-ONE

Luke

BECKY'S ALARM WENT OFF, and he reached over to shut it off. Between the news of her father, her mid-evening nap, and then the girls coming over, she'd barely gotten any sleep the night before.

He hadn't slept at all, had just held her in his arms and waited for her to pull away.

Her father. Him. The two men who'd been the closest to her had wounded her deeply. How could she possibly trust any man ever again? How could she trust *him?* Those thoughts had twisted around in his head for hours, and he knew, just fucking knew, that sooner or later his Becky was going to come to her senses and ask him to go.

Or kick his ass to the curb.

Both of which he deserved.

Fingers on his cheek startled him. He glanced down into the eyes of the woman he loved.

Fuck, he loved her so much.

"Morning," she said softly.

"Morning," he managed to croak back.

Blonde brows pulled together, gray eyes studied him intently. "I've been thinking."

They were soft words. Pitying words.

Luke's gut sank, twisting itself into knots, knowing that the moment he'd spent all night worrying about had come to fruition. He'd hoped for a few more days, maybe weeks, but perhaps this was for the best. A clean break.

Clean. *Ha.* He was about to be sliced to the core.

"I understand," Luke told her before she could give him his brush-off. "I'll go back to Texas, give you plenty of space when I'm in town—"

"What the fuck are you talking about?"

He shook himself. "Me. Your father. We're pieces of shit who don't deserve any part of you. I should leave you to your life and—"

Two palms gripped his cheeks. "Shut. Up." She tilted his face so their foreheads touched, her breath hot on his lips. "This is the first and last time I'm going to say this, okay? We both have our demons, and we're both fucked up in our own special ways, but you don't get to sacrifice yourself because you have a hero complex." She shook him slightly. "What happened to you fighting for me?"

He brushed her hands off his face, pushed up from the mattress. "Since I spent the whole night reliving all the ways the men in your life have hurt you. And *I'm* one of them, Bec. You're better off without any of us and—"

"It's Becky," she snapped. "And I didn't fall in love with you because you're really good at shouldering guilt and beating yourself up. I fell in love with you again because you're sweet and protective and make me laugh. Also, your tongue is fucking brilliant, and that thing you do with your index finger should be illegal." She stood and poked him in the chest. Hard. "So don't shit on that love by reverting back to being the martyr. We've moved beyond that. Remember?"

Fuck.

She was right.

"*Of course*, I'm right." She glared, and he realized he'd spoken aloud. "I need you in my life, Luke. You make it . . . better." A roll of her eyes. "I know that's pathetically unromantic, but the truth is that you make *me* better, you love me for who I am, and I—I'm not just going to let you go because you've developed a sudden streak of nobility." Those eyes that had rolled a heartbeat before now glistened with tears. "You promised you'd fight for me, for us. How can I trust in that if you're going to give up and walk away because you think I'm better off without you? Newsflash"—she smacked him—"I'm not. I want you in my life. But you've got to be *all* in. Because you doubting yourself and us, thinking it's best to just leave at the first sign of adversity, that's not good for either of us."

Luke dropped his chin to his chest. "I'm sorry."

"How do I know you're not going to be *sorry* again the next time something bad happens, huh? How do I know you're going to stay for—" She swallowed. "Forever. Because I want you. *Forever*. I want a future, regardless of this shit with my father and our past. I love you. I want *you*."

His heart was pounding, his throat was tight, his eyes burned like hell.

Because he wanted that, too.

He wanted Becky forever.

"Damn," he said. "I'm really fucking this up."

"Yeah, you are."

His lips twitched. "You should also know that despite this talk, I may still occasionally be a fucking idiot—"

"Occasionally?" she muttered.

"Frequently," he amended. "But I do usually learn from my

mistakes." He met her gaze. "I'm sorry, sweetheart. I wish I could say that my idiocy was from lack of sleep. But nope. It was my own mind that had convinced me I needed to leave you in peace. That and my exceedingly guilty conscience."

"Well, stop it," she said. "Stop feeling guilty for things that happened a decade ago. Let's worry about now. And our future."

Future.

Luke liked the sound of that a lot.

"You love me, sugar pie?" he asked, sliding his arms around Becky and pulling her close.

"Against my better judgment, I seem to have fallen for you again."

"My subliminal programming worked then."

She snorted. "Dork."

"*Your* dork."

"I'll take that."

"Should we go back to bed for a while?" A beat. "Or all day?"

"I like the sound"—she yawned—"of that. I'll text my boss. I've never used a sick day in my life," she said. "Today seems like a good day to start."

"I like that plan," he said, lifting her up into his arms. "I feel like I should apologize for being an idiot again."

"Please don't, Pearson," she said snuggling close to him as he tucked them both back under the covers. "Remember that whole communication thing I mentioned before? Let's chalk this up to that. You had a concern, you voiced it, and we moved on."

"And you told me that you loved me."

"Pft. As if that were ever in question. I've loved you since the night of prom."

"What? Why?" he asked. "All I was thinking about was how desperate I was to feel you up in that red dress."

"Because." She pressed a kiss to the spot just above his heart. "Most boys would have been mad I decided to ditch them the night before the dance to go with my friends. But instead of getting huffy or angry, you spent the whole night dancing with my friends, making sure we all had a good time. I knew it then."

"Knew what?"

"That you were special."

"Fuck, Becky."

She pushed up to see his face. "What?"

"You undo me."

Returning to snuggling, she said, "I know."

"And modest, too," he teased, running his fingers lightly up and down her spine. "So, are you going to tell me now?"

"Tell you what?"

He wound a strand of her hair around one finger. "What I interrupted earlier, what you've *been thinking*."

"Oh."

A tug of that blonde lock of hair. "Oh? That's it?"

"I shouldn't tell you, just out of principle."

"Principle?" he asked.

"For making me get all ramped up and preachy at six in the morning." She sniffed. "I should make you *suffer*."

Luke shifted his hips. As usual, just holding her had made him hard and aching.

"I *am* suffering."

Snorting, she said, "I was thinking about the dates. We have five left, by my calculations."

"Should I make some quip about lawyers being bad at math?" She glared and he lifted his palms in surrender. "Never mind. Five dates left is right."

"Well, I was thinking about just skipping to date ten." Her

fingers drew nonsensical shapes over his chest. "Or to the part that came after date ten." She pressed another kiss to the place above his heart. "To the part where I say I don't want you to leave."

"Oh."

"Oh?" she teased, throwing his words back at him. "That's it?"

He laughed, stealing her lips in a kiss that he hoped conveyed how much he loved this woman. "That's it," he told her when they broke for air, chests heaving. "I don't care about the numbers. I just know I want forever with you."

"Is that so?"

"I think I've made that more than clear."

She wove her hands into his hair, tugged his mouth down to hers again. "Well, make it clear again."

Done.

He pressed his lips to hers, nipping the corner of her mouth, sliding his tongue along hers in the rhythm they both liked best. Her body was flush against his, soft to his hard, lean curves fitting perfectly into his boxier shape. He loved the feel of her in his arms, of her mouth tangling with his, the slight tug of his hair when he was kissing her exactly right.

"I don't . . . care when," he said, gasping in air and trying pathetically to make the words semi-coherent. "When . . . we do it, but I"—he sucked in a breath—"I need to give you Date Ten."

She frowned.

"Promise me."

"To do what?"

"To go on Date Ten with me."

A shrug, her brows draw together. "Okaay. I promise to go on Date Ten with you?"

"More question than affirmation, but I'll take it," he said.

Becky rested her head on his chest and, as was their habit,

they lay quietly in bed, each lost in their own thoughts. Luke liked that they were creating new habits, and he didn't hate the fact that she was close to him.

Eventually, however, she pulled away, reached for her cell, and sent off a quick text.

Then she sighed and pushed off him.

"I think it's time I see my dad."

Luke wanted to tell her, "Fuck no." He wanted to protect her from whatever the bastard might say or do.

But this was *his* Becky.

She didn't need him to fight her battles for her.

She needed him by her side, to help her if she stumbled, and to be ready with a hug—and maybe a bottle of wine and a box of It's-Its—if things went to shit.

She needed a partner, not a savior.

And Luke finally thought he could be that for her.

So, instead of telling her she shouldn't go, he held her hand on the drive over to the hospital. Instead of demanding to accompany her, he asked if she wanted him there, and when she *did* want him by her side, Luke quietly slipped his arm around her waist as they entered her father's room and saw the frail man in front of them.

Too thin, cheekbones in sharp relief, but the man's gray eyes showed him to be undoubtedly related to Becky.

A woman, thin and blonde, who would have been beautiful if not for the pale skin and reddened eyes adorned by huge dark circles, sat at his bedside. She stood when they entered, but Becky hardly noticed.

"Dad?" Becky asked, horror in the greeting.

TWENTY-TWO

Bec

IT WAS TERRIBLE.

So much worse than she'd imagined.

He couldn't look like this, couldn't be *this* sick. Not when he'd always seemed larger than life, boisterous, domineering. She remembered him being able to captivate a room just by uttering a few choice words.

Now he looked as though he couldn't even squish an ant.

"Rebecca?" he asked.

"Hi, Dad," she murmured.

"Why are you here?"

Blunt words, sharpened to wound. The woman next to him, a slender blonde with a pretty face and kind eyes and who was, presumably, Helen, her father's new wife, gasped. "*Ronald.*"

Luke squeezed Becky's hand.

"Good to see you too, Dad," she said, lifting her chin and crossing over to the bed. "Thanks for returning my phone calls."

Helen frowned, searching through her purse for a moment before extracting a cell phone. "I'm sorry. I didn't realize—"

"I wasn't referring to today," Bec told her, "so much as over the last twenty years."

"O-oh." Helen's gaze dropped to her hands. "I meddled." A sigh. "I shouldn't have."

Bec touched her arm. "I'm glad you did. This is a conversation we need to have, as much as *Ronald* has tried to avoid it."

"You shouldn't be here, Rebecca."

"Because you can't stand the sight of me? Or because you didn't want your new wife to know just how much of an asshole you are?"

Another gasp from Helen.

"Sorry," Bec told her. "I should have warned you, my father and I don't get along. Though that mostly stems from the fact that he abandoned me and then wouldn't return my calls for twenty years."

Helen glanced from Bec to *Ronald*, eyes searching both of them for long moments.

"Is that true?" she finally asked.

Bec's father looked away, and suddenly that anger inside her, that rage twisting and wounding and *hurting* so fucking badly was just . . . gone. In that empty cavern, resignation took its place.

She was never going to get what she wanted.

"Unfortunately, it is true," Bec said. "I'll spare you the sordid details, but know that for the last twenty-odd years I wanted nothing more than to have a relationship with my father. Ask him how many times I called or emailed, how I went to his office once a month for fucking years trying to see him, but he was always too busy. Ask him how he never wished me a happy birthday or merry Christmas—"

"We're Jewish," her father interjected.

Bec lifted one brow. "Happy Hanukah, then?"

"You haven't changed," her dad snapped. "You still want too much."

Bec's eyes dropped to the floor, hurt washing over her and making her wish for the empty feeling from a few heartbeats before.

But then Luke was there, slipping a reassuring hand around her waist, tugging her close. "No," he said. "She's never wanted enough for herself. She deserves so much more—"

"It's okay," she said, love taking the place of hurt. Love for this man that somehow made even the shittiest version of a family reunion better.

His emerald eyes darkened. "No, it's fucking not."

She squeezed his hand and he squeezed back, giving her the strength to face her stepmom. "The truth is that after my mother died, not once did my father reach out to me. I was the horrible painful secret, locked away and disapproved of. *I* wasn't worthy of Ronald's fucking attention because I wasn't my mother, was I?"

Gray eyes so much like her own drifted to the window, stared out. "No. No, you weren't her. Could never be her."

Her all-encompassing anger might have left her, alongside the emptiness and most of her hurt, but a lot of her spiked armor had flown the coop along with those emotions, and so, Bec wasn't going to lie—hearing those words stung.

"Well," she said, lifting her chin, shoring herself up. "Good to know nothing's changed. I'll leave you to your—"

Movement at the door caught Bec's gaze. Luke shifted to let someone pass by him and Bec turned fully, watching a pretty brunette walk into the room. The woman was much younger than her, maybe a college student or recent grad, but she moved with a confident grace, as though she'd been striding across hospital rooms for a long time.

And, after seeing the state of her father, Bec thought, maybe she had.

The shift in the room at her entrance was palpable.

Tension twisted the air. Helen jumped to her feet, moving to place herself between Bec and the girl.

"Mom?" she asked. "Dad? Is everything okay?"

Punch.

To Bec's heart. Her gut. Her brain.

Somehow, she'd known it was coming, and yet the blow was almost physical.

But Luke had her, his warm hand on her spine centering her, understanding in an instant that she could have withstood almost anything aside from this.

Bec's father had moved on without her.

Replacement wife. Replacement daughter.

Helen laced her arm through her daughter's and led her back to the door. "Why don't you go find your brother? Get us some coffee from the cafeteria?" She glanced at Bec. "Just some coffee and some food, okay?"

Bec had been doing okay until—

Okay, fuck it all, she'd been barely hanging on. She felt as though she'd been treading water in the open ocean for hours, and now a shark had decided to swim on up and chomp on her leg.

Brother.

Yeah, that fit.

Somehow, it all fit.

She ignored her half-sister leaving and instead turned back to her father. He *had* to feel something—shame, sadness, disappointment. But as she stared at him, Bec discovered that she couldn't find any trace of those emotions.

Instead, there was . . . nothing.

Aside from the same unique color of their eyes, they might have been perfect strangers.

And, if she were facing facts, they *were* strangers.

Bec glanced up at Luke. "I'm ready to go now."

Fury had tinged the tops of his cheeks with pink, but to his credit, he only nodded and took her hand.

"I'm sorry," Helen murmured. "I didn't know . . ."

Bec managed a half-smile. "It's—I—" She shook her head, wanting to find some absolution. This wasn't Helen's fault. She seemed like a nice woman who'd been trying to do the right thing.

But in the end, the words wouldn't come, so Bec just averted her eyes and let Luke lead her to the door.

She paused on the threshold, glanced back one last time at her dad. "I hope you found what you were looking for."

Her father's voice was still the same, even if his body wasn't.

It trailed after her into the hallway.

"I didn't," he said. "But I'll be with her soon enough."

Bec squared her shoulders and lifted her chin and walked with Luke to the elevators, but at the last minute, she tugged him into the stairwell and sank down onto the top step, resting her head on his shoulder.

She wanted to cry, but couldn't. Instead, she just sat there and sighed, despondent and aching and . . . just so *fucking* disappointed

"The people who have the most power over you also hold the greatest ability to disappoint," Luke said, and when she glanced up at him in surprise, he shrugged. "Something my therapist once told me."

"Yeah," Bec agreed. "I think he got it right on that one."

The barest hint of a smile on his lips. "You okay?"

"No." Another sigh. "But I will be. I just wanted—" She broke off.

"The perfect ending." He brushed a hand down her hair. "I'm sorry. You deserved that perfect, storybook ending. You deserved to have your family be there and—"

"He's not my family," Bec said. "I've made my own."

Luke nodded, pressed a kiss to the top of her head. "The girls *are* awesome."

"You, too, you know that, right? You're my family, too."

His lips curved. "I think you mean, I've weaseled my way back into your life, and I'm not leaving."

Her own smile teased the corners of her mouth. "More like a fungus, growing under the surface until one day it pops up and"—she clicked her tongue—"fucking mushrooms everywhere."

Luke laughed, hugged her tight. "As long as I'm a fungus without a cure, then I'll take it."

"As if you'd be any other kind." She chuckled. "Look at us, so romantic, talking of fungi and weasels after an emotional scene at my father's deathbed. If this isn't in a rom-com, it definitely should be."

"I can get behind that."

"Ew."

He squeezed her again. "Sorry, poor word choice." Then he bent and whispered in her ear. "But I thought you liked it when I got *behind* you."

She giggled.

Luke joined her for a few moments before sobering. "I am sorry, though. Sorry he couldn't be what you needed."

"Me, too," Bec said. "But what I'm realizing is that sometimes the people you need the most just don't have it in them to fulfill that role, and you either have to move on or find it in yourself."

"Sweetheart," he whispered. "That's really . . ."

"Deep?" She smirked.

He frowned. "I was going to say incredible."

"Damn, and take away my chance to insert another innuendo into this conversation?"

"Apparently." His lips twitched, and he tugged her to her feet. "Come on, let's get out of here. If we're playing hooky from work, we may as well do it right."

"Now *that* I can get behind."

And somehow, despite the last hellish half hour, Bec managed to walk out of the hospital with a smile on her face.

She knew the wounds under the surface wouldn't heal as easily, but for the first time in a long time, she was okay with that. No scrambling for armor or running or pushing people away.

She could just be.

And live.

She wanted to do that, too.

LATER THAT NIGHT, she filled in her friends, via video chat this time, since she and Luke were cuddled up in bed.

"I'm not going to lie," she said, after they'd all commiserated about asshole parents. "Aside from the dad stuff, it felt really good to not be at work today."

"And the sex," Abby said with a cackle. "I'm guessing the sex felt really *good*, too."

Luke laughed, and she smacked him.

"You," Bec said into her laptop, "are as bad as I am." A beat. "And I like it."

They all laughed.

"But seriously," she told them. "You guys mean the world to me."

"So many feelings," Heather said. "Hot damn."

Abby sniffed. "I'm sending you a virtual hug."

"We love you, Becky," CeCe said.

Rachel smiled. "I second that statement."

"We're family." From Sera and, yeah, that was exactly right.

"Thank you," she told them. "For everything."

"Thank *you* for letting us drink more wine," Abby joked. "We're using you for the free booze."

They all laughed, and then CeCe cleared her throat. "Um, actually, I'm not going to be able to partake in your free alcohol for a while." She paused, a smile growing on her face. "For seven more months, actually."

Five voices, including Bec's, rang out in excitement. Shrill excitement if Luke's wince was any indication.

"Oh, my God," Abby said. "You're going to be such a great mom!"

"I don't do the diaper thing," Heather said. "Don't forget that, m'kay?"

"Congrats, CeCe. I'm so happy for you guys," Rachel added.

Bec smiled. "I'm looking forward to you bossing McGregor around."

CeCe laughed. "Are you kidding? The man's already been hovering like a busy little bee. He'd be jumping through flame-covered hoops at the smallest sign of any bossing on my part."

"You need to take merciless advantage," Abby advised sagely.

They all giggled.

"You guys are terrible, but I love you anyway." CeCe grinned. "And I'm only taking a *little* advantage. Colin's been bringing me copious amounts of croissants since it seems to be the only thing I can keep down."

CeCe talked for a few more minutes, regaling them with humorous renditions of Colin's protectiveness before she yawned and they all bullied her off the phone with orders of a mid-afternoon nap. Abby's son, Carter, popped his face into the screen a second later, demanding a hug and consoling after a nightmare, and so she hung up. Then Sebastian came home, so Rachel signed off, and Heather was kissed off the line by Clay, who, quite literally, kissed her to distraction before pushing the button to disconnect.

"And then there were two," Sera joked ominously.

"You okay?" Bec asked.

"I'm great, actually," Sera said. "I got a new client today. He's some sort of tech genius who's looking for a new place. Wants something private and on the coast." A shrug and even through the phone line, Bec couldn't shake the feeling that her friend was sad. "Which means, expensive. Of course, it also means a better commission for me, so . . ."

"Win-win."

"Yup. Exactly." Sera smiled, but it was off.

Definitely sad.

"Salads tomorrow?"

She shook her head. "Can't. I'll squeeze myself into your calendar next week."

"Okay," Bec replied. "Get some sleep, okay? You look tired."

"Always so sweet to me." Sera reached a finger for the screen.

"Your turn's coming," Bec said, taking a stab at what was bothering her friend. It had to be hard to see everyone else happy and paired off. Even if Sera weren't jealous, exactly, it still had to sting that she was alone when her friends weren't. "If *I* could find Luke, your Prince Charming has to be just around the corner—"

"Yeah." But her tone betrayed her.

Sera didn't believe Bec.

"Hey—"

"Night." Sera disconnected.

"Damn," Bec said. "I hate that she's lonely."

"She has you guys," Luke reminded her, closing the laptop, and setting it onto the nightstand. "And she's special. Someone will recognize that someday."

"They have to see through the superficial surface layers first."

"They will." He tugged her down, kissed the top of her head.

"How do you know?"

"I saw through you, didn't I?"

EPILOGUE

Luke, six months later

IT HAD TAKEN six long months to finally get his Becky out for Date Ten.

Right after her single day of hooky, she'd taken on a huge case, and any extraneous date nights had gone by the wayside.

But, unlike the past, Luke hadn't been jealous of her career. He'd missed her like crazy, of course, but he'd dealt with her long days at the office by pulling some long days of his own. His renewable energy cells had been rolled out, and as expected with new technology, there had been plenty of problems to deal with.

There had been many nights of dueling laptops on the coffee table after he'd officially moved into Becky's place and after they'd *communicated* and figured out that she could do some of her casework at home.

Maybe it wasn't traditional couple time, but Luke just liked being with her.

And he especially liked the times that their laptops got tossed to the side and Becky straddled him on the couch.

Yeah.

Those were great times.

But now her case had wrapped up . . . or rather, the opposing lawyers had accepted her proposal and settled, and so she was taking two whole days off.

They were driving up to Tahoe to hit the slopes the following day, but tonight?

Tonight was Date Ten.

Or maybe Date Ten Thousand, but semantics didn't matter.

He'd wanted to do this for Becky forever.

He just hoped his instincts were right and she'd be into it.

"How fancy is this restaurant?" she asked, striding into the room.

And fuck him six ways to Sunday, but she was wearing the dress.

The. Dress.

The fucking red dress from prom and it was . . . everything.

She'd slipped on one of those short sweaters that just covered her shoulders and partway down her back, but the rest of it—skintight red silk, breasts spilling up and over the deep V, slit up to her thigh.

Fuck it all. He wanted to forget Date Ten.

"Uh-uh, mister," Becky said, bending to slip on a pair of sky-high black heels and nearly making his eyes bug out of his head. Her breasts. Her legs. Her *ass*. "I somehow managed to squeeze into this dress. You're not getting it off me that quickly."

Luke made a garbled sound.

Maybe agreement? Maybe disappointment?

But he did manage to get his head out of his ass long enough to pull the black velvet box from his suit pocket.

Becky stopped several feet away, glanced at the case—too large for a ring—then down at herself.

"You are *not Pretty Woman*-ing me."

Luke closed the space between them. "So what if I am?"

"How did you even know that was my favorite movie? I don't think we've ever—"

"Oh, we've discussed movies. You've just never confessed your fondness for Richard Gere."

"It's Julia Roberts," Becky said. "Her smile is incredible."

"*You're* incredible."

One hand came to her hip. "Okay, Mr. *Incredible*. Nice try. Tell me how you found out."

"I know *everything* about you." But he felt his lips curving, knew the cat would soon be out of the bag.

Becky glared. "Sera! She gave up the goods. How dare—"

He opened the box. It held a necklace and earrings. Not diamond ones like from the movie, but opals because his Becky loved opals.

Probably because they were unique and changeable and looked like they were filled with fire.

"*Oh.*" She reached a finger as though to touch the necklace then glanced up with a glare. "Nice try."

He pretended to make the lid chomp her fingers. "Gotta do it right." Then he set the box aside and carefully slipped the necklace out. He fastened it around her neck before handing her the earrings. "Want to do those?"

She nodded, and he trailed her into the bathroom as she used the mirror to swap out the earrings she was wearing for the new ones.

"So," he said, nerves making his hands shake. "I'm not saying I lied, because we *are* eating at a very fancy restaurant. It's just that *after* the eating part we're going to the symphony. Or a version of it." His words came a little faster as he hurried to explain. God, he'd been building this up in his head for so long, thinking that she would love it. But what if she didn't? What if she actually hated it? "I know it's not *exactly* like the movie, but you told me a long time ago that you always wanted to watch a movie that had a live orchestra playing the score. And they're doing *Pretty Woman* tonight, and I thought—"

She stepped into his arms, squeezed him tight. "I *fucking* love you."

Luke released a relieved breath.

"But I told you about wanting to see a movie like that a long time ago." She stepped back, met his stare. "Like *ten* years ago."

He grinned. "So maybe Sera gave up the goods a long time ago. *Like ten years ago,*" he said, mimicking her voice.

His Becky huffed and started to say something—okay, he had to face facts, it would be sass—and so Luke kissed her. He was probably smearing the sexy as shit red lipstick she wore, but he found he didn't give a damn about her lipstick when her mouth was on his, when their tongues tangled, when those gorgeous breasts were flush against him.

"You sure you don't want me to peel this dress off you?" he asked when they broke away, chests heaving.

"Nice try," she said and reached a hand up to wipe the lipstick from his mouth. "This dress is staying on." She grabbed a tissue, blotted her lips, then reapplied the color before brushing by him and strutting out of the bathroom. "At least until *after* the movie."

Yeah, he thought, watching her luscious backside sway as she strode for the front door, *he could live with that.*

"Stop ogling my ass, Pearson," she tossed over her shoulder. "I'm hungry."

Yeah, he could live with that, too.

Fire tempered with sweet and plenty of sass.

Luke knew he wouldn't want to *live* any other way.

Thank you for reading! I hope you loved meeting Luke and Bec! The next book in the Billionaire's Club series is BAD FIANCE. Find out how Sera finally gets her HEA, even though it might not the happy ending she was hoping for...

CLICK HERE TO READ BAD FIANCE NOW >

And if you enjoyed BAD DIVORCE, you'll love the sexy, stubborn, and wonderfully nosy Gold Hockey crew. The first book in the series, BLOCKED, is free to download!

"Off-the-charts hot, smexy scenes with one of the best book boyfriends I have come across!" —Amazon reviewer

Her life was a disaster...Don't miss the hilarious Life Sucks series, starting with TRAIN WRECK. Derek Cashette was determined to salvage the train wreck of her life...and she was just as determined *not* to let him be the hero.

DOWNLOAD TRAIN WRECK FOR FREE >

I so appreciate your help in spreading the word about my books, including sharing with friends! Please leave a review on your favorite book site!

You can also join my Facebook group, the Fabinators, for exclusive giveaways and sneak peeks of future books.

SIGN UP FOR ELISE FABER'S NEWSLETTER HERE: https://www.elisefaber.com/newsletter

Excerpt from BAD FIANCE

Sera was going to lose her mind.

Or throw a fucking tantrum.

And see? There it was. A curse word.

Seraphina Delgado did *not* curse. It wasn't seemly or lady-like, and . . . she was a thirty-something-year-old woman who still saw her mother's disapproving face in her mind when she dared to utter a curse word.

Well, know what?

Fuck. Fuck. Fuckity-fuck.

There. *Ha.*

Mental diatribe somewhat satisfied, Sera turned to the source of her wannabe tantrum.

Tate Conner.

Tech genius. Real estate client—

Or, rather, *former* real estate client because he was a giant pain in her as—*tush.*

Congrats, Mom, she thought. *I sound like a four-year-old.*

But Tate Conner had become a *former* client because he *was* such a pain. He didn't like anything, he never showed up for appointments. In fact, she'd lost count of how many times he'd *forgotten* about a scheduled showing after number twelve.

So yeah, she'd kissed away any hope of a giant commission and had told Tate they wouldn't be working together.

That had been four months ago.

And now he was here in her office, looking all . . . Tate-like.

Super helpful description, she knew, but it just wasn't fair. Weren't these tech guys supposed to be nerdy and unattractive? Because Tate Conner *definitely* didn't fit in with that description.

He was tall and lean, but strong. En route to one of the appointments he'd actually made, Sera had gotten a flat tire. She'd managed to get her car to the house then had called Triple-A and Tate had shown up as the man had struggled with her lug nut—poor phrasing, but not the point. Anyway, he'd approached the tow truck driver, had tweaked the angle of the wrench, and the nut had popped right off.

Again, more poor phrasing, but—

Sera mentally shook herself.

He'd claimed it was all about leverage, but she'd seen the way his muscles had rippled under his T-shirt. He was strong, and it was more of a natural strength rather than a result of spending loads of time in the gym.

And the worst part? Besides the whole strong and as tall as her—hard to do considering she was over six feet—Tate was also pretty.

Really pretty.

A chiseled jawline, a straight nose, lips that were totally kiss-able, and a pair of dimples that made the rare appearance. He also had the prettiest blue eyes she had ever seen and sandy blond hair that was more at home on a surfer than an executive.

That hair had been her undoing.

And as she always did, Sera had fallen in love.

Fallen fast. Fallen hard.

For a man who had absolutely zero interest in her.

Her friends—none of whom ever dreamed about finding their happy endings and several of whom had been decidedly against them, she felt required to point out—were all married or paired off. Abby had babies. CeCe was due any day, and—

Sera was alone, pining after a man who'd created the latest social media craze.

Yup. Her life was *ah-maz-ing*.

Tate cleared his throat, and Sera realized she'd been staring at him dumbfounded for a good couple of minutes.

"I'm sorry, Mr. Conner." She stood, forced herself to shake his hand. "I was wool-gathering."

Sparks. The moment their skin touched, she felt *actual* sparks.

Just like every other time before.

And just like every other time before, she was the only one affected.

He smiled—eliciting more sparks, because her body was a stupid jerk—and said, "I've been known to do that from time to time."

Sera indicated for him to sit in the chair in front of her desk as she sank into her own chair. He continued to stand, but she started talking anyway, desperate to get this conversation over with. "How can I help you today?" she asked. "I do hope"—*Do hope? What was she, British? Ugh*—"I-uh . . . I hope you were able to find a house. The agents I passed along are very good at finding unique properties, and I even gave them a few locations to start with . . . " She bit her lip, attempting to stop the ramble.

"No."

Just no.

Um. Okay.

He lifted a hand, rubbed the back of his neck. The movement made his shirt lift, exposing several inches of flat stomach and tan skin and, oh God, a trail of blond hair leading south. Her mouth watered, desperate to trace that path with her tongue—

Sera sucked in a breath, popped to her feet.

"Ah. I'm sorry." She picked up a random file, pretending to know what was in it. "I'm actually really busy, so this will have to continue another time."

Like never.

She rounded her desk, forced a smile. "Mr. Conner," she said when he didn't move. "I'll have my assistant schedule something soon."

"Seraphina."

She shivered at the sound of her name on his lips—soft, a

little raspy, and deep enough to conjure up all sorts of unhelpful fantasies in her mind.

Shaking herself, she moved to open the door.

Suddenly, Tate was there, hand over hers, body inches away, spicy scent inundating her senses.

Sera's breath caught. "What are you—?"

He seemed to be arguing with himself then finally, those piercing blue eyes locked onto hers. "I need you to marry me."

—Bad Fiancé out now!

Want a free bonus story? Hate missing Elise's new releases?
Love contests, exclusive excerpts and giveaways?
Then signup for Elise's newsletter here!
https://www.elisefaber.com/newsletter

And join Elise's fan group, the Fabinators https://www.facebook.com/groups/fabinators for insider information, sneak peaks at new releases, and fun freebies! Hope to see you there!

BILLIONAIRE'S CLUB

Bad Night Stand

Bad Breakup

Bad Husband

Bad Hookup

Bad Divorce

Bad Fiancé

Bad Boyfriend

Bad Blind Date

Bad Wedding

Bad Engagement

Bad Bridesmaid

Bad Swipe

Bad Girlfriend

Bad Best Friend

Bad Billionaire's Quickies

Did you miss any of the other Billionaire's Club books? Check out excerpts from the series below or find the full series at https://www.elisefaber.com/all-books

---

Bad Night Stand
Book One
https://www.elisefaber.com/bad-night-stand

Abby

"I'M THE BEST FRIEND," I said and lifted my chin, forcing my words to be matter-of-fact. I'd been through this before. "You might be fuckable to the nth degree and perfect for Seraphina, but I refuse to set her up with a liar."

In a movement too quick for my brain to process, my stool was shoved to the side and I was pinned against the bar, heavy hips pressing into me, a hard chest two inches from my mouth.

Seraphina whipped around at the movement and I could just see her over Jordan's shoulder, her blue eyes concerned.

"Hi, Seraphina, I'm Jordan," he said, calm as can be, gaze locked onto my face then my eyes when mine invariably couldn't stay away. "I'm going to borrow your friend for a minute."

"Abs?" she asked, and I knew she'd go to bat for me right then and there if I needed her to.

"Weasel or no?" I managed to gasp out. For some reason, I couldn't catch my breath.

Not that it had anything to do with Jordan.

No, it had *everything* to do with him.

"Weasel?" he asked.

I shook my head, focused on my best friend. Weasel was our code name for the men trying to weasel, quite literally, their way into my pants and then into hers.

I was just about ready to say fuck it—or me, rather—even if Jordan was a Weasel. He smelled amazing. His body was hard and hot against mine.

And it had been way too long since I'd had sex.

"No chemistry on my part—" Seraphina began.

"Your friend isn't who I'm attracted to," Jordan growled out. "You are, and it's fucking pissing me off that you don't believe that."

—Get your copy at https://www.elisefaber.com/bad-night-stand

Bad Breakup
Book Two
https://www.elisefaber.com/bad-breakup

CeCe

"You're even more beautiful than I remember," he said, and the rough edges of his accent hacked at the words, making them more of a growl rather than a soft sentiment.

Her breath caught, and she found her eyes drawn to the stormy blue of Colin's.

And she stared again, utterly entranced before she remembered how it had all ended.

Her in a white dress.

Alone, except for the priest who'd given her a pitying look and invited her to stay as long as she needed.

But it had always been like this, Colin's gruff words winning her over. They were unexpected from him—he was typically so reserved and taciturn. And that compliment, freely given as it was, chipped away at any defenses she managed to erect.

The problem was that his words weren't always followed up by action. In fact, they were typically trailed by pain for her and fury for him.

The hurt of those memories—of Colin so angry, her so broken—helped shore up her resolve.

"Don't say things like that," she snapped and started to pop her earbuds back in. Her friends at home had filled her phone with a slew of romantic audiobooks and she decided that she much preferred fictional heroes at the moment.

At least if they broke their heroine's heart, it was only once.

Colin had already broken hers twice.

She wasn't looking for a round three.

—Get your copy at https://www.elisefaber.com/bad-breakup.

Bad Husband
Book Three
https://www.elisefaber.com/bad-husband

Heather

"I'm getting drunk," he said, but allowed her to pull him inside the car so that her driver could shut the door behind them.

"You're already drunk," she said.

He stiffened. "*More* drunk."

"Fine," she said, half-worried he was going to launch himself from the sedan. She'd never seen Clay like this. Usually he was so cold and uncompromising, impenetrable even under the toughest of negotiations. He was . . . well, he was typically as *Steele*-like as his last name decreed.

She wrapped her arm through his in order to prevent any unplanned exits from the vehicle and gave the driver the name of her favorite bar. "If you really want to drink, let's do it right."

And *then* she'd drop him at his hotel.

Except it didn't happen that way.

Yes, they hit the bar.

Yes, they drank.

Yes, they got plastered.

But then they woke up . . . or at least, *Heather* woke up.

Naked.

With a softly snoring Clay Steele passed out next to her in bed.

That wasn't the worst part.

Because Heather woke up naked and with a softly snoring Clay Steele in her bed *and* she was wearing a giant diamond ring on her left hand.

Still not the worst part.

That came in the form of a slightly crumpled marriage certificate tucked under her right cheek.

And not the one on her face.

She pulled it from beneath her, a cold sweat breaking out on her body, dread in every nerve and cell.

She *still* wasn't prepared for the horror she found.

The marriage license had been signed by . . . Heather O'Keith and Clay Steele.

Holy fuck, what had she done?

—Get your copy https://www.elisefaber.com/bad-husband.

Bad Hookup

Book Four
https://www.elisefaber.com/bad-hookup

Rachel

Rachel watched her boss dance with her second husband—or maybe husband twice over was a better description?—and gave a little sigh of happiness.

Yes, Heather was technically her boss, but she was also her friend.

And her friend deserved a happily ever after.

The party was just getting started, friends and business associates spilling out onto Heather's back patio that had been decorated with twinkly lights, an abundance of flowers, and plenty of portable heaters.

Only the Sextant—herself, Abby, Bec, Seraphina, CeCe, and Heather—along with Jordan and Colin, Abby and CeCe's husbands, respectively, and of course, Clay, knew that the surprise wedding they'd celebrated that night was technically a *second* wedding.

The rest of the guests just thought Heather had pulled a fast one on Clay.

Rachel smiled as she remembered the way the couple had come down the stairs, both of their eyes a little damp, but love emanating from every fiber of their bodies.

The vows had been beautiful and—

Ugh. She was getting a little too sappy.

Wiping the tears away before they could escape—and heaven forbid, ruin her mascara as Abby was always so worried about—Rachel blew out a breath and set about making sure the food the caterers had delivered was arranged properly.

Soon the cocktail hour would be over, and then the group of fifty-plus—okay, so she knew it was exactly fifty-*seven* guests, because she was damned good at her job—would descend like locusts on the food tables.

Everything needed to be ready.

So, she went down her mental checklist. Appetizers. Check. Several types of salad. Blegh, but check. Entrees. Pasta, chicken, and vegetarian. Check. Check. Check. The cake was also ready, perched at the end of the table and waiting to be cut.

"This little shindig your doing?"

Rachel froze, all her nerve endings going on alert.

She knew that voice.

She knew if she turned around, she would see *him*.

Him.

Tall, much taller than her, but lean when compared to her curves. Still, all that lankiness hadn't meant a lack of strength. He'd been all sorts of hard and hot as he'd pinned her against the door and pounded into her.

Rachel cleared her throat but didn't rotate to face him. "Not my doing. I just helped out."

A long pause, probably because normal people usually looked each other in the eyes when they conversed.

"Well, from what I've seen, you've done *a lot* of helping out." He put a hand on the table next to her, and she shifted away, shivering. She remembered what those fingers could do, how they'd traced over her skin, slipped between her legs, slid *inside*.

Shuddering, she smoothed out a wrinkle on the tablecloth.

"For a last-minute surprise wedding, everything is beautiful," he said, no doubt waiting for her to say something semi-coherent.

She didn't.

Instead, Rachel shrugged and began fussing with the placement of the warming dishes.

The man didn't take the hint. He didn't leave.

Why won't he leave?

She dropped her chin to her chest.

"So," he finally said after another lengthy—and silent—moment. "Gay, taken, or not interested?"

"Oh my God," she moaned, one hand coming up to push her bangs off her forehead. "This is *not* happening."

"I—" A beat then his voice was incredulous. "I *know* that moan." Warm fingers grasped her wrist, tugged until she could see him in all his yumminess.

Her moment of weakness. Her hookup because she'd been feeling desperate and lonely and—

"It's you," he said softly.

Yes, it was *her*. Rachel, the good girl who didn't sleep around, who *certainly* didn't hook up with random strangers in a bar.

Rachel, who *had* hooked up with a stranger.

The sex had been damned good. Incredible, actually.

But it had been just that. Sex. And she hadn't been able to let go of the guilt. She'd now slept with a grand total of two men in her life, and one of them was her husband.

"I—" She tugged at her wrist. "I need to go." ·

Heather and Clay chose that exact moment to saunter over.

Why universe? Why?

"Rachel," Heather said, closing the distance between them and hugging her tight. "I told you not to work so hard on the wedding. This"—she swept her hand around the deck—"is all too much."

"You deserve to have a beautiful wedding," Rachel murmured to her boss and gave her a quick squeeze before she stepped back.

Heather shook her head, but she was smiling. "Thank you."

"Yes, thank you," Clay said. "For all of it. I know it was a lot of work, but we appreciate—*Oh, good*"—he wrapped an arm around her shoulders, turning her to face Sebastian fully—"I was going to introduce you two, but I guess you've already met my assistant, Sebastian."

Sebastian's expression flickered with shock—no doubt mirroring her own—but luckily, Clay and Heather were too lost in each other and the moment to recognize just how big of a bomb Clay had just dropped.

After a few more words, their bosses moved on to talk with a business associate, and Sebastian's blue-gray eyes darkened. His stare, all heat and desire and sex appeal, was what had undone her the first time they'd met.

But it was his words, the hint of a growl edging into his voice that made her insides tremble in *that* moment.

"I'm *really* looking forward to working with you, Rachel."

She tipped over a bowl of salad dressing.

—Get your copy at books2read.com/BadHookup.

Bad Fiancé
Book Six
https://www.elisefaber.com/bad-fiance

Seraphina

Sera was alone, pining after a man who'd created the latest social media craze.

Yup. Her life was *ah-maz-ing*.

Tate cleared his throat, and Sera realized she'd been staring at him dumbfounded for a good couple of minutes.

"I'm sorry, Mr. Conner." She stood, forcing herself to shake his hand. "I was woolgathering."

Sparks. The moment their skin touched, she felt *actual* sparks.

Just like every time before.

And just like every time before, she was the only one affected.

He smiled—eliciting more sparks, because her body was a stupid jerk—and said, "I've been known to do that from time to time."

Sera indicated for him to sit in the chair in front of her desk as she sank into her own chair. He continued to stand, but she started talking anyway, desperate to get this conversation over with. "How can I help you today?" she asked. "I do hope"—*Do hope?* What was she, British? *Ugh.*—"I-uh . . . I hope you were able to find a house. The agents I passed along are very good at finding unique properties, and I even gave them a few locations to start with . . . " She bit her lip, attempting to stop the ramble.

"No."

Just no.

Um. Okay.

He lifted a hand, rubbed the back of his neck. The movement made his shirt lift, exposing several inches of flat stomach and tan skin and, oh God, a trail of blond hair leading south. Her mouth watered, desperate to trace that path with her tongue—

Sera sucked in a breath, popped to her feet.

"Ah. I'm sorry." She picked up a random file, pretending to know what was in it. "I'm actually really busy, so this will have to continue another time."

Like never.

She rounded her desk, forced a smile. "Mr. Conner," she said when he didn't move. "I'll have my assistant schedule something soon."

"Seraphina."

She shivered at the sound of her name on his lips—soft, a little raspy, and deep enough to conjure all sorts of unhelpful fantasies in her mind.

Shaking herself, she moved to open the door.

Suddenly, Tate was there, hand on hers, body inches away, spicy scent inundating her senses.

Sera's breath caught. "What are you—?"

He seemed to be arguing with himself then finally, those piercing blue eyes locked onto hers. "I need you to marry me."

—Get your copy at https://www.elisefaber.com/bad-fiance

Bad Boyfriend
Book Seven
https://www.elisefaber.com/bad-boyfriend

"Who is it then?" she asked through stiff lips.

Because it couldn't be. Her brother didn't know about them. She'd made sure of it. They'd kept things on the down-low and . . . then she'd nursed her broken heart two thousand miles away in college.

"Tanner."

Her gut twisted.

Double fuck.

And a shit for good measure.

"That's fine, right?" Bas asked. "You guys seemed to get along great." Concern rippled across his face. "Is there something wrong. Did—"

"No," she said quickly. "That's great. I'm sorry. I'm just preoccupied with my new project."

He grinned. "Always work with you."

She blew him a kiss. "You know it."

"Great. So you'll be paired up with him. And I know it's been a while, but he's coming into town next week to catch up." He tapped the roof of her car, took a step back. "You want to grab dinner with us?"

"I'd love too," she lied before getting into her car and with a wave that hopefully didn't show her dismay, Kelsey drove away.

Paired up with Tanner.

Been there, done that.

Got the souvenir broken heart.

Triple fuck.

—Get your copy at https://www.elisefaber.com/bad-boyfriend

ALSO BY ELISE FABER

Breakaway

Breakout

Checked

Coasting

Centered

Charging

Caged

Crashed

A Gold Christmas

Cycled

Caught (February 1,2022)

Breakers Hockey (all stand alone)

Broken

Boldly

Breathless

Ballsy (April 26,2022)

Love, Action, Camera (all stand alone)

Dotted Line

Action Shot

Close-Up

End Scene

Meet Cute

Love After Midnight (all stand alone)

Rum And Notes

Virgin Daiquiri

On The Rocks

Sex On The Seats

Life Sucks Series (**all stand alone**)

Train Wreck

Hot Mess

Dumpster Fire

Clusterf*@k

FUBAR (March 29,2022)

Roosevelt Ranch Series (**all stand alone, series complete**)

Disaster at Roosevelt Ranch

Heartbreak at Roosevelt Ranch

Collision at Roosevelt Ranch

Regret at Roosevelt Ranch

Desire at Roosevelt Ranch

Phoenix Series (**read in order**)

Phoenix Rising

Dark Phoenix

Phoenix Freed

Phoenix: LexTal Chronicles (**rereleasing soon, stand alone, Phoenix world**)

From Ashes

In Flames

To Smoke

ABOUT THE AUTHOR

USA Today bestselling author, Elise Faber, loves chocolate, Star Wars, Harry Potter, and hockey (the order depending on the day and how well her team -- the Sharks! -- are playing). She and her husband also play as much hockey as they can squeeze into their schedules, so much so that their typical date night is spent on the ice. Elise is the mom to two exuberant boys and lives in Northern California. Connect with her in her Facebook group, the Fabinators or find more information about her books at www.elisefaber.com.

f facebook.com/elisefaberauthor

a amazon.com/author/elisefaber

BB bookbub.com/profile/elise-faber

instagram.com/elisefaber

g goodreads.com/elisefaber

P pinterest.com/elisefaberwrite

How To Salvage
more! Millions
From Your Small Business

by

Ron Sturgeon

3rd Edition
Published by Mike French Publishing
Lynden, Washington

Edited by Paula Felps & Eric Anderson
Cover Design: Kris Crawford,
Mike French Publishing of Lynden, Washington
Interior Design: Mark Tank, Printers Plus & Dwayne Parsons

Licensed in The United States, China, Korea,
Russia, and The Czech Republic

Published by
Mike French Publishing
1619 Front Street
Lynden, WA 98264
Phone: 360-354-8326   Fax: 360-354-3013
Email: Mike@MikeFrench.com

This publication contains the opinions and ideas of its authors and is designed to provide usefull advice to its readers on the subject matter covered. Any reference to people, companies, products or services does not constitute nor imply an endorsement or recommendation unless so stated within the text. The publisher, the collaborator and the authors specifically desclaim any responsibility for any liability, loss, or risk either financial, personal or otherwiese which may be claimed or incurred as a consequence, directly or indirectly, from the use and/or application of any of the contents of this book in this or any subsequent edition.

The publisher does not attest to the validity, accurancy or completeness of this information. Use of a term in this book should not be regarded as affecting the validity of any trademark or service mark.

For reseller information including quantity discounts and bulk sales, please contact the publisher.

Library of Congress Cataloging-in-Publication Data

Sturgeon, Ron.
  How to salvage more millions from your small business / by Ron Sturgeon. -- 3rd ed.
    p. cm.
  Rev. ed. of: How to salvage millions from your small business. c2002.
  Includes index.
  ISBN 978-0-9717031-4-8 (alk. paper)
  1. Small business--Management. 2. Success in business. I. Sturgeon, Ron. How to salvage millions from your small business. II. Title.
  HD62.7.S893 2009
  658.02'2--dc22
                                    2008041423
Manufactured in the United States of America

10 9 8 7 6 5 4 3 2 1
Third Edition